Call Me Yours

Enchanted Hierarchy

Love, Fey

This is a work of fiction. Names, characters, places, and incidents are either the product of the author's imagination or are used fictitiously, and any resemblance to actual persons living or dead, business establishments, or events is coincidental.

Call Me Yours

Published in the United States of America
First Printing, 2026

No part of this work was created with the use of AI.
Cover Art by Amanda Webb
Chapter Header Images by Love Fey
Scene Break Images by Love Fey

Dedication

To all the book girlies out there who once pretended they were a fairy. I'm sure you never imagined a demon bodyguard, so I've got you covered. 😉

Author's Note

Dear Reader,

Call Me Yours, featuring Thatch and Aster, takes place during the same timeline as *The Line Between*, Case and Paisley's story. You can read *Call Me Yours* even if you haven't read *The Line Between*, but it will spoil some very important moments with Case and Paisley, and it'll obviously reveal the climax of their story.

Between these pages, you will come across references to Case and Paisley and their unique relationship, and see glimpses of it, but that's all that I do, because this story is dedicated to Thatch and Aster.

With that said, I truly hope that by the time you finish *Call Me Yours* that I've intrigued you enough to read *The Line Between*, if you haven't already. There's so much goodness in that story, including their true ending that's not revealed here, and that's why I fully believe it'll be an experience for you, dear reader, whether it's read before or after *Call Me Yours*.

Now, I'll stop babbling so you can get to the most adorable demon and fairy couple.

Love,

Fey

Content Warning

Call Me Yours is a paranormal bodyguard romance. All of the sex scenes involve a demon (male main character) and a fairy (female main character), and those scenes contain detailed descriptions and language.

Below is a more thorough list of what you will encounter between the pages of this novel. Keep in mind that these are the main content warnings and may not cover smaller warnings that are specific from reader-to-reader. Take care, dear reader.

Explicit Language
Graphic Sexual Content
Masturbation
Fellatio
Cunnilingus
Sex Toy Play
Vaginal Sex
Bullet Wounds
Blood
Threats
Burn Injury (not the MCs)
Kidnapping (off page)
Characters are Unalived (not the MCs)

If these are okay with you, please proceed.

Happy reading!

1

Rosemary & Lavender

"Aster, come meet your bodyguard."

Jittering with nerves, Aster stepped around the door to come face to face with the demon whom Lord Case had tasked with protecting her. Paisley, her best friend, had just been crowned the vampyre-faye queen, and in retaliation a fairy had been murdered, her wings cut from her back. Aster was a fairy, and Case wanted to make sure she didn't succumb to the same fate. While he protected Paisley, Aster would be his right-hand's charge. She imagined a huge, brutish demon with a hideous face and horrendous mannerisms. Truthfully, she didn't know all that many demons. Lord Case was the first, and he'd surprised her with his beauty and kindness. She had no idea what to expect from this demon who'd be her bodyguard. Certainly, she didn't expect the demon standing beside Case.

Yes, he was huge, but not in a brutish way. He was tall, a few inches shy of Case's magnificent height, but this demon's body was wider in the shoulders, which matched the large horns that extended on either side of his head. Those horns curved like those of a great buffalo. Not that she'd ever seen a buffalo in person before, only in books. The width of his upper body slimmed down the length of his body to lean hips and long legs.

She'd never harbored an inkling of attraction to any creature before, but looking at his hips, encased in black pants, she felt a stirring in the pit of her stomach. It was strange, startling, and it made her squirm in place.

The demon before her had violet skin. She didn't know that a demon could be such a shade. Perhaps that was her own ignorance or prejudice, but this demon's skin was beautiful. He had black hair that was pulled behind him, out of sight, and navy-blue eyes that met hers, and with it, she was hit with a feeling that she didn't understand. It was far more than attraction—longing.

Her own eyes widened. "Oh my."

The demon grinned. "Hi there, baby doll." His voice was deep but gentle.

Aster's cheeks warmed. *Baby doll*?

First, Case started to call her cutie pie, an affectionate name among, she hoped, friends. But this? This 'baby doll' from this demon? It was affectionate in a vastly different way. Before she could contemplate the nickname further, the demon lowered to a knee in front of her, braced an arm across his chest, and laid his fist over his heart. "I will lay my life down for you. You have my word."

Aster gaped. Was he serious? Her gaze shifted to Paisley, who was also gaping at the demon. Aster didn't know what to say to such a declaration, to such a demon, so she said the only thing that came to mind. "Th-thank you."

Paisley cleared her throat as Aster stood there, about to burst into flames from the heat rising in her body. "Aster, why don't you show Thatch and Case into the parlor? I'll make us coffee."

That sounded like a good thing to do right about now. A distraction. So, Aster headed toward the parlor. After a few steps, she peered over her shoulder to see the violet demon following her. She sat sideways on the small couch, so they'd be able to talk, and patted the cushion next to her, inviting him to join her. He lowered onto the other half of the couch. The added weight had her tipping toward him. She sucked in a breath when her breasts brushed his muscular bicep.

"I'm sorry," she whispered and scooted back.

"No, I'm sorry. I'm not meant to fit on something so small and delicate." Their knees were touching, although they were on opposite sides of the couch. "I'll sit elsewhere." He started to rise, but she stopped him with a hand on his knee.

"No, please stay. You're fine where you are. I don't mind. Really."

He settled back into place.

"I didn't catch your name earlier. What is it?"

"Thatch."

"Thatch is a—"

"A fairy name. I know. Paisley already said that."

"I was actually going to say that it's a beautiful name."

"Not half as beautiful as the name Aster."

Her cheeks were warm again, no doubt revealing to Thatch what his words were doing to her.

"Aster is a flower, isn't it?"

"It is. Traditionally, fairies are named after flowers or something in nature. Like a thatch."

"I'm no fairy, baby doll. Far from it."

But his skin was a lovely shade of violet, just like violet flowers, just like the color of her own hair. And his hair, as black as onyx, was fashioned in a long, single braid that stretched down his back. He might not be a fairy, but the Goddess had blessed him nonetheless.

"Can you tell me about flowers?"

Thatch's question surprised her. What demon would want to know anything about flowers? "What do you want to know about them?"

"Anything, everything."

She looked toward the shallow bowl of crimson roses sitting in the center of the coffee table. "Well, roses probably have the longest history and the deepest roots throughout many cultures and traditions, from the very first one that ever bloomed. They're sacred to many deities, and even mortals consider them to be the most significant of flowers. Rose petals and rose hips have been used medicinally for ages. They can be used in teas to calm anxiety, and they can be worn to guard against the evil eye." She spotted a tiny rose bud in the shallow bowl and plucked it free. "May I?"

His brows lowered. "May you what?"

She pointed to his hair.

He blinked. "Oh, um, sure."

She pulled his braid over his shoulder and found his hair to be the softest she'd ever felt before. Not even another fairy's hair had ever felt this soft. She slipped the rosebud into the tie at the end of his braid. "There. Now you're protected."

"I'm here to protect you, baby doll. Not the other way around."

"Well, why can't we protect each other?"

He didn't say anything to that, only stared into her eyes while she continued to touch his hair. She released his braid, and it slid behind his shoulder like a silk rope. She cleared her throat. "Each rose color has its own special meaning." She indicated at the crimson roses. "Red is for love, romance, passion"—she met his eye—"desire."

His wide chest lifted as he inhaled.

She plowed on. "Pink is for admiration, gratitude, and happiness. Yellow…friendship. White…innocence and purity. Even the number of roses that someone gives is significant. One is…" She paused. "Um…one is 'love at first sight.'"

He tilted his head, and her blasted cheeks heated again.

"Three, as you can imagine, means 'I love you.' Ten means perfection. Twelve is a statement…a request…'be mine.' Do you have a lucky number?"

"I do. Nine."

Her heart skipped a beat. "Eternal love."

They were silent a moment, staring into each other's eyes.

Suddenly Thatch said, "Your eyes."

She blinked.

"What color are they?"

"Lavender."

"Tell me about lavender."

"Many cultures burn it to purify, cleanse, and protect. It can help with sleep and ease anxiety and bring about an overall calm."

He was gazing into her eyes when he said, "I can see that. What about violets?"

She smiled. "A sign of innocence."

His navy-blue gaze followed her hair from roots to tips. "That's fitting."

She cleared her throat again to get her next words out. "And is it fitting for you?"

"I don't know if anyone would ever call a demon innocent, but I do my best."

Except, there was something so innocent about this large demon next to her. She broke eye contact and studied her hands settled in her lap, her hands that itched to touch his hair. "Violets also symbolize everlasting love and have been gifted as a declaration to always be true. Medicinally, they are used for breathing problems. Although they are small and delicate, they are quite powerful."

Thatch's voice was lower when he asked, "And asters?"

"Asters have always been thought of as an enchanting flower."

He nodded slowly.

"They are a talisman of love and a symbol of patience."

He took a slow breath.

"Their leaves have been burned as an incense to keep serpents away."

She didn't know why she said that. A useless fact that he'd never need to know. Unless Lord Case's mansion became overrun with snakes. Unlikely, but if that ever happened, he'd know how to get rid of them naturally.

Paisley walked into the parlor then and set a tray of cups and a pot of coffee on the small glass table. "Help yourselves."

Aster chose a cup from the tray and set about making her coffee. Anything to distract herself from the handsome demon beside her, but that was impossible as she stirred in sugar and cream, turning her coffee into a milky-white, sweet concoction. Thatch picked up a cup next. It appeared so tiny and dainty in his hand, and it made Aster smile. Her smile grew when she watched him do the opposite of her—a tiny stream of cream and zero sugar.

Across from them, Paisley and Case were bickering about coffee, but Aster wasn't paying attention to their words because she was transfixed by Thatch's hands. Violet and big but so gentle around that porcelain. She wondered what they'd feel like on her skin, and that thought mortified her. She knew nothing about any of that stuff—holding hands, kissing, sex. Nothing. Nada. She was as innocent as violets represented.

"Paisley is going to come with us to search the grounds."

Case's announcement to the room caught her attention and drew her from her embarrassment. If Paisley was going…

"Then I'm coming, too," she said.

Paisley whipped toward her. "Absolutely not."

"Like hell," Case snapped.

Their refusal to allow her to help sent a rush of anger through her. She leaned forward and set her cup on the coffee table with a rough hand. Any harder and that porcelain would've cracked. "I may be small, but I am capable. I'm her lady-in-waiting. Before you, it was my job to stand beside her and protect her. Where she goes, I go."

Paisley and Case didn't say anything.

Next to her, Thatch shifted. His right knee slid along the outside of her thigh, pushing up the hem of her dress by an inch. She was staring at his knee and her rumpled dress, and feeling her heart racing in her chest when Thatch said in a deep voice, "I will keep her safe." She gazed up to him. He was looking at her, too, and the way he did had her shivering.

Case let out a breath of annoyance. "Fine. I guess we're a search party."

Thatch sat forward, picked up Aster's cup of coffee, and handed it to her. She took it, and their fingers brushed. The touch had them peering into each other's eyes again. Where their fingers had grazed, her skin now tingled with awareness.

While sipping her coffee, she stole peeks at him. He was simply the most handsome creature she'd ever laid eyes on, and he was stealing peeks at her, too. Could he be feeling the same things? It was selfish, but she hoped so.

Coffee cups drained, the four of them ventured outside to search for the body that belonged to the severed fairy wings. The very thought that a fairy had been murdered so close made Aster shiver in fear.

A large, warm hand curved over her shoulder. "Are you okay?"

Concern clouded Thatch's eyes.

"Yes." She didn't want any of them to know she was scared, especially not after she'd demanded to join them. For Paisley, she needed to be strong.

The large, warm hand left her shoulder. As soon as it was gone, she wished for it back. Thatch's hand had such a kind touch, and it made her feel safe.

They walked, none of them saying a word. Aster searched tree roots and nearby bushes for the limbs of a small body similar to her own. She didn't want to find a body, but if there was a dead fairy in these woods, they deserved to be laid to rest properly, and she'd assist with that. Her gaze swept over the forest floor.

Birds twittered overhead.

Beneath their shoes, twigs snapped and pine needles crunched.

A thick bush of stinging nettle lay ahead, and Thatch was heading right for it. Stinging nettle could be quite irritating to the skin, and she didn't want him to feel any discomfort, so she laid her hand on his wrist and pointed at the wild bush. "Careful. That's stinging nettle."

"I gather that it stings."

"It does, indeed. Although, maybe…maybe it wouldn't bother you. I don't know how a demon may react to stinging nettle. You might not even notice it."

He smiled. "It's unlikely to faze me."

She lowered her head. "Right. Of course."

His fingers curled around her chin, and he lifted her head so that she'd meet his eye. "But thank you for your concern. I appreciate it." His thumb grazed over her cheek when it burned with embarrassment. So quick the touch was before his hand disappeared. "Tell me about

stinging nettle. Does it do more than sting?"

"Oh yes, stinging nettle actually makes a nice, mild tea that can ease fevers and head colds. The sting, though, can be beneficial, too, and relieve joint pain."

They passed an overgrown bush of yarrow that strangled the trunks of several pine trees.

"And these?" Thatch asked, pointing at the delicate, white flowers.

"Yarrow. They have been used throughout creature and human history to heal wounds and stop blood flow. When dried, they can be made into a poultice and applied directly onto wounds. Small, but mighty, they've saved many lives."

A bee buzzed past and settled on a nearby plant. "Red clover," she said. "They make the most delicious teas. Do you like tea?"

"I haven't had much of an occasion to drink tea."

"If you're going to be around, I can make you tea some time."

"I'm going to be around, baby doll. Every day, every night, I'm going to be around."

She knew she was blushing, and she couldn't stop it.

"What are those? They're pretty."

She looked to see a bush bursting with spears of purple. "Oh, that's lavender. You've never seen lavender before?"

He shook his head, so she went over to the bush, broke off a bloom, and held it out to him. Their fingers brushed when he took it. He lifted the flower to his nose, making her smile. "Is this what you smell like?"

Such a question. She squirmed nervously. "I…I don't know."

Suddenly, his fingers were cupping her chin again, and he was raising her head so that she stared into his eyes. His touch—so tender, so soft—had her own eyes widening. Gaping up at him, she lifted her hand and slipped her fingers into his palm. Emotions she'd never felt before tightened in her throat and had her heart thudding in her chest. It almost felt violent the way it pounded. Thatch was like pollen, and she was a thirsty bee. His touch, his gaze, she yearned for both and more that she didn't dare hint at that she desired.

Thatch held the lavender bloom next to her temple. He studied her for several heartbeats before he finally said, "Your eyes really are the same color."

She nodded.

His hand lowered, and she pulled her fingers from his palm. That same hand pressed to the small of her back and ushered her forward with the lightest of touches. She continued after Paisley and Case, but she noticed that Thatch didn't let the lavender bloom fall to the ground to be plucked up by a bird or to decompose into compost. He held it carefully.

She caught the scent of rosemary and plucked a sprig from a bush. "Lavender and rosemary go well together," she said while stroking her index finger down the length of the fresh sprig. "They can be dried and tied together for cleansing bundles. Rosemary vanishes negativity and dark forces while lavender calls in the good."

Thatch asked question after question about lavender and rosemary, and she answered each one, forgetting why they were out there in the first place.

Until Paisley shouted, "Get down!"

Bark exploded off the tree in front of Paisley, showering her and Case with wooden shrapnel.

Fear had Aster tugging her wings close to her body. Before she could drop to the ground, strong arms swept her off her feet and encased her in a fierce hold. She was in the crook of Thatch's body, low to the ground, when she saw Case jolt and a splotch of blood appear on the back of Case's shirt. She'd never seen someone get shot before, but she was witnessing it now while bullet after bullet peppered Case's back.

Her friend.

Her friend was getting shot in front of her while protecting her sister.

She couldn't help it; she screamed in horror.

2

The Fairy Swing

T

Aster's scream cut through Thatch, slicing him with fear. If anything happened to her, he'd go on a rampage because only that would suffice harming such a delicate, lovely creature.

Case launched into the air, taking Paisley with him.

Thatch hooked Aster's legs with his arm and shot toward the treetops with her cradled to his chest. Her fingers gripped his shirt, and she shook against him. For that alone he wanted to cause whoever was doing this pain. Fairies shouldn't ever be afraid. It was a crime against nature. And one of them had been murdered so close to where Aster lived and slept. The thought that someone could want to do to her what they'd done with the fairy somewhere in those woods increased his rage. No one would touch her. He'd sworn to Aster, and he vowed it to himself now; on his life, no one would touch her.

He landed on the cobblestone in front of Case's mansion and set Aster gently to her feet, but he didn't want to completely let her go, so he held her shoulders as she sobbed.

Paisley broke free of Case and rushed over to Aster. "Are you okay?"

Aster sniffed. "It's not me."

Paisley whipped around to Case.

While they argued, Thatch stroked a hand down Aster's back, hoping to calm her. She shifted closer to him, and his chest clenched. He'd had no intention of falling for the fairy Case charged him to guard, but upon first sight, something had happened. Love at first sight wasn't supposed to exist for demons and fairies, but, Diablo, it'd happened. Whether the universe or the Enchanted Hierarchy agreed with it or not, he'd fallen for a fairy the moment he'd laid eyes on her, and he wasn't going to let anyone or anything take that away from him.

Except, this wasn't the first time a demon and a fairy had fallen in love, and he doubted it'd be the last.

Case met his eye, and he nodded, telling his boss and best friend that whoever had done this would pay and pay dearly. His nod had Case leaping toward the sky. Thatch stepped back from Aster and catapulted after him. They flew back to Paisley's property, on a mission to hunt down the people who'd riddled Case with bullets, intending to take out the vampyre-faye queen.

Eyes peeled, they took opposite sides of the forest and created zigzagging patterns while searching for the culprits. Thatch couldn't detect so much as a subtle movement. Not a flick of wings. Not a flash of color. There certainly wasn't a giant around. Whoever had done it had escaped before they'd returned. Likely as soon as they'd dispensed the final bullet into Case's back.

Unsuccessful, they returned to Case's.

"Now what do we do?" Thatch asked.

"I'm still thinking that through."

He followed Case to the door. Halfway there, he realized he'd crushed the lavender bloom that Aster had given him in his hand. The petals were stuck to his palm. He dusted them off, scattering the tiny purple petals over the steps as he neared the door.

When they stepped inside, Aster's gaze jumped to them, and she sighed. "They're okay."

Paisley, however, sprang to her feet and attacked Case, demanding for him to remove his shirt so that she could tend to his wounds. Thatch wanted nothing more than to go to Aster, where she shivered on the couch, but Paisley asked him for supplies.

"I'll get what you need." He gathered up forceps, a clean towel, a bowl for the bullets, and a stool. In the foyer, he found Paisley and Case standing before a painting and talking closely. When Paisley saw him, she marched back into the parlor, ordering Case to follow.

Thatch laid out the equipment she'd need to remove the bullets from Case's back and stepped away, sensing that she wanted to do this. Case got those bullets intended for her, and she'd dig each one out herself. Thatch knew better than to get in her way, so he joined Aster, where he really wanted to be anyway. He sat on the couch, which was fashioned to fit demons like him, and resisted the urge to take Aster into his arms.

Across the room, Paisley spat at Case, "Eight fucking bullets. If you weren't already injured, I'd hurt you myself."

Case's reply had Thatch groaning. "You can hurt me later, baby. In my bedroom. With a whip, chains, riding crop. Whatever you'd like. I'm game."

"Diablo," Thatch muttered.

Beside him, Aster giggled.

His gaze cut over to her. Her head was dipped and her gaze trained on her lap, not on Case who was half naked. For that, Thatch could at least be thankful. If she were to look at any demon's half-naked body, he wanted it to be his own.

A few tiny purple petals clung to her forearm. When he'd carried her, he must've crushed the mangled lavender bloom against her arm and nearly embedded the petals into her skin from how tightly he'd held her. He plucked them off one by one.

She watched him place each petal in the center of his palm.

There were nine.

Eternal love.

Did she notice?

Her gaze shifted to his.

Behind them, Case growled in pain.

Aster turned back to Paisley and Case as Paisley removed a bullet from his back.

"Is it iron?" Aster asked.

"Only one way to find out." Paisley held the bullet between her thumb and forefinger. A hissing sound and a thin stream of smoke slipped out from between her fingers.

Case plucked the bullet from her. "These bullets would've been deadly to you. Even one."

They would've been deadly to Aster, too. That fact had Thatch edging closer to her.

Paisley's voice drew his attention again. "Aster, do you think you have enough fairy dust with you to heal him?"

Aster hopped to her feet. "Yes."

She removed the bundle that she wore at her hip, opened the drawstrings, and dipped her slender fingers inside. Her attention was fixated on Case's back, and the most beautiful granules of sparkling light trickled from her fingertips. When the fairy dust touched the bullet holes, their glimmer increased like fragments of starlight. Then the bullet holes vanished.

While no one looked, Thatch gathered the lavender petals in his palm and stashed them in his pocket. He intended to keep them. Even when they shriveled up and dried.

Case rotated on the stool, lifted Aster's hand to his lips, and kissed her knuckles. "Thank you, cutie pie."

The action, the words, and Aster's blush had a flash of jealousy pulsating through Thatch. It was unfounded. Case was all about Paisley, and Thatch could recognize that whatever Case felt for Aster was innocent, but Thatch couldn't stop the feeling of possessiveness that overtook him.

"I have to go to the faye faction."

Paisley's announcement had Thatch pushing to his feet, because that meant she'd be leaving, and so would Aster. The queen may not want Case following her around, but Thatch would do whatever necessary to keep Aster safe, and a bodyguard would never let his charge out of sight.

"So, it's time that Aster and I—" Paisley's words halted in her throat when Case picked her up. "What are you doing?!" Even though her voice was raised, her legs still came around Case's waist in a move that was purely sexual.

Case carried her out of the parlor. "I still need nursing. From you."

"Put me down!"

"What? You think they don't know we fuck? Trust me, they know."

Thatch shifted awkwardly. "Diablo."

"Well, they certainly do now, you idiot!"

Aster giggled under her breath again.

Thatch peered at her. "We should, um, we should get out of here before they start." The last thing he wanted was to hear the two of them bang each other.

Aster's wide eyes settled on him. "Is it safe to go outside?"

"You'll be safe with me, baby doll. I promise."

"Okay."

He held the door open for her, and she stepped outside. They walked silently for a moment. Her presence calmed him and overwhelmed him all at once.

He yearned to be near her, but her closeness made him nervous because he wasn't used to this, desiring someone so completely that it stole his breath from his lungs. Was this some sort of fairy magick? The way he wanted to fall to his knees in front of her, bare his soul, worship her, and beg her to feel something, even just a smidge of what was consuming him?

The need to do something for her that would make her fairy heart smile became a driving force, and a thought came to mind. "I have something I want to show you. Do you mind taking a walk in the woods again? I promise nothing will happen to you. Case's property is guarded."

She nodded, and he took her hand.

Neither of them spoke as he led her down a path in the woods, away from the mansion, to a spot he'd discovered a couple of years ago. Aster's wings fluttered on her back. He wished he could decipher what that meant. They were so beautiful, her periwinkle-blue wings, and so fragile-looking, like transparent tissue paper. He stiffened when he'd recalled what he'd done to the lavender bloom when he'd grabbed her to him. Had he crushed her wings in the same way? Diablo, he'd never forgive himself if he'd hurt her. Never.

"Your wings. I'm not used to wings that are always out." His own wings he could tuck into his body when not in use, but fairy wings did no such thing. "I didn't hurt them when I held you earlier, did I?"

"No." She squeezed his hand. "You didn't. I'd moved my wings to shield myself before you grabbed me." She turned around to demonstrate. Her wings dropped down, so that the tips pointed to the ground, and slid over each other as they flattened to her back. Then they sprang back into place.

Thatch couldn't help it; he reached out and traced the sloping side of her right wing with the tip of his finger. He smiled when she shivered. "They're so delicate."

"Fairy wings are deceptive." Her voice was a

whisper. "They're stronger than you may think."

"Much like you, baby doll."

She shook her head. "I'm not strong. Paisley is strong. But me?" She shook her head again.

"You stood up to Lord Case and demanded to join us to search for a dead body. That takes courage. Willing to be around a strange demon also takes courage." He skimmed his fingers over her wings' sheer, periwinkle-blue majesty. "They're beautiful."

"Th-thank you."

Would she always stutter a 'thank you' to him? He hoped that one day she'd thank him for his compliments and not stutter.

She turned. "But you're wrong. It doesn't take courage to be around you. You're not a scary demon, Thatch."

"I've never wanted to be." He'd worked his whole life to be different. He didn't curse. He didn't drink. He didn't sleep around. Although it hadn't done him any good. Until now. With this sweet fairy gazing up at him without an ounce of trepidation. "Come on, baby doll. It's just ahead." He folded his hand around hers again, and there was no hesitation in her steps as she walked beside him. "Periwinkles are flowers, right?"

"Right."

"Tell me about them."

"Well, they're linked with death."

He jerked. "What?"

"They tend to grow in graveyards, covering grave plots. Lore claims that if you pick one from a grave, you'll be haunted. Elsewhere, they are a source of protection. The leaves had once been stuffed into the mattresses of newlyweds to encourage marital fidelity,

love, and passion."

"Interesting flowers."

She snorted. "Indeed."

They came into a clearing, and Aster pulled up short. A gasp floated from her parted lips. A magnificent tree stood tall in radiant beams of sunlight. From a thick, sturdy branch, flowered vines twined around each other and stretched toward the ground where the vine hovered a few feet above the dirt.

Aster's voice was soft when she said, "It's a fairy swing." She left his side. At the swing, she trailed a hand down a braided vine. "This is amazing."

"I found it a while ago."

She stood on the other side of the swing and peered at him through the flowering ropes. "Not just anyone can come across these, Thatch. Like fairy circles, these are protected, hidden. For you to find this, that means something."

He stepped up to the swing. "What could it mean?"

"That you're special, and Mother Nature has chosen you."

"For what?"

To love a fairy, perhaps?

She lifted a slender shoulder.

"Sit down," he said. "I'll push you."

She lowered onto the vines.

He took the ropes in his hands, pulled her back, and then released the swing. Her hair flew behind her like a cape when she swung forward. His hands touched the middle of her back when she returned to him, and he pushed her forward again. A laugh like nature's music floated into the air. The higher he pushed her, the more she laughed.

Hearing that sweet laughter made him chuckle, too. Demons didn't usually have cause to laugh in such a way, but he'd wager that none of them had heard a fairy's happy laughter or had been the reason for such a lovely sound.

A breeze swept past them when he pushed Aster on the swing. With it, the breeze carried a scent that swirled around him, knotting him up with its fragrance. He'd never smelled anything more intoxicating. The swing brought Aster back to him, and he pushed her forward once more. But that smell had him like a hook. It was delicious, luring him in with each inhale. When she came back, his hands caught her hips, stopping her midair.

She gasped from the sudden jolt.

"What's that smell?" he demanded, his voice rougher than intended.

"I'm sorry." She was breathless from laughing. "When I'm happy, my scent becomes stronger. If it's too much for you—"

He looped an arm around her waist to hold her to his chest and swept her hair from her neck. Then he settled his nose in the crook between her ear and shoulder and took a long, slow inhale, drawing that luscious scent deep into him. “Diablo, you smell good.”

She shivered in his arms. The desire to feel her shiver for him again and again became overwhelming. He caressed her neck, gliding his thumb up and down her throat. “What kind of perfume is this?”

“I…I’m not wearing perfume. That’s just me.”

“Just you?” He groaned. “There is no ‘just’ about the way you smell. It’s—” He shook his head, brushing the tip of his nose against her neck. “If I could smell this every day…” He hadn’t meant to say that out loud, but he certainly hadn’t expected her reply.

“You can.”

He wanted that, but she wasn’t his to want or to lay any sort of claim to. That painful fact had him releasing her. The swing took her away from him. She let out squeal. The swing reversed, and he wondered, was she right? Could Mother Nature have selected him? Did Mother Nature know his secret? Something he’d never even told Case?

He swallowed down the secret and laid his hands to Aster’s back, sending her flying with the swing. Her laughter rang through the air.

After several minutes, she climbed off the swing and they walked back to the mansion, taking their time. Thatch had no idea how long Case and Paisley would take. Fortunately, when they returned, the two of them were waiting downstairs.

Paisley moved away from Case. “Aster, say goodbye to your bodyguard. We’re going home.”

Thatch spun toward Case. “Is that wise?”

"Case doesn't make my decisions for me," Paisley said, her voice biting. "I have work to do at the faye faction. Whether Lord Case likes it or not, I'm leaving."

Thatch met her eye. "Whether you like it or not, wherever she goes"—his gaze flicked to Aster—"I go."

Paisley eyed him a moment before sighing. "I suppose I wouldn't be able to stop you, now would I?"

He shook his head. Absolutely zero chance.

"Alright, well, Case and I are going to have dinner tonight."

Paisley's announcement had Aster clasping her hands together in sheer glee.

"So," Paisley continued, ignoring Aster's delight, "you and Aster can have dinner together."

Now Aster fidgeted, oozing mortification.

"Come on then," Paisley said. "You can keep Aster company."

He nodded once. "I can do that."

On the way out the door, Case caught his arm and whispered in his ear, "I intend to keep Paisley here all night, so you'll have plenty of time to cozy up with that adorable creature."

If Case weren't the demon lord, Thatch would slug him for that one.

3

What Women Want

The rest of the day, a head count took place at the faye faction, and the missing fairy was discovered—dead in her home, wingless. The very thought of it sent chills through Aster's own wings. Paisley and Aster, with Thatch standing guard outside the room, readied the fairy for her burial ceremony. Then the faye faction came to get her to finish the burial preparations.

Now it was dinnertime and Paisley was leaving in a red dress that would undoubtedly give Case a heart attack. Or an instant boner. Or both. At the same time.

On the balcony, Aster watched Paisley fly away. Then she stepped back inside to where Thatch waited. "Should you follow her? Make sure she gets to Case's safely?"

"If she doesn't show up in two minutes, Case will go looking for her. Besides, she doesn't let anyone see her wings. She wouldn't have let me follow."

That was true. Paisley was insecure about her wings after being bullied over them her whole life. Aster was the only one privileged to see them.

Aster stared at Thatch a moment. They were going to be spending the evening together. Alone. She barely knew him, but she couldn't stop herself from jittering when he returned her gaze. Clearing her throat, she asked, "What would you like to have for dinner?"

"I'll eat whatever you put in front of me."

"Do you know how to cook?"

"If I didn't, I'd starve."

"Would you like to help me?"

"I would."

In the kitchen, she handed Thatch a flowery apron with lace on the edges. "I'm sorry that I don't have anything more…demon-y."

He grinned. "Demon-y?"

"Well, I didn't want to say manly."

He folded the apron in half and tied it around his waist. "How do I look?"

She bit her bottom lip. With his black pants, white button-up shirt, and that silly apron tied around his lean waist, he was outrageously handsome. A demon wearing an apron with a flower print and frill? She never would've been able to imagine it, but here a demon was in a flower-print-and-frill apron, willing to cook in a fairy's kitchen, and looking devastatingly handsome while doing it. "You look…you look good."

His lips quirked at the corners. "What do you want me to do first?"

"Wash your hands."

Now he broke out in a full-blown grin.

"I don't mean…I didn't mean to…it's just that washing hands is the first step." She would never have meant to cause offense. Especially not to a demon.

"Aster, baby doll, I know about cooking hygiene. Consider my hands washed." He went to the sink and lathered up.

She followed suit before checking the stocked fridge for a meal they could make. There was a bright pink, fresh slab of salmon on a silver tray waiting for herbs and garlic. While mostly vegetarian, she did eat fish every once in a while. When she started to pull it out, Thatch took it from her and set it on the counter. One by one, she removed vegetables from the crisper—asparagus, cherry tomatoes, onions, and bundles of mustard greens, kale, spinach, and romaine lettuce. Every time, Thatch stole each one from her hands and laid them out for her. Never mind the fact that they weren't heavy in the least. His attention to her was foreign and left her speechless. She'd never had a bodyguard before. Maybe this was standard practice; don't let your charge do anything that you can do for them.

Side by side, they chopped veggies, pan seared salmon, mixed a sauce, and tossed greens. Then they were sitting across from each other at the dining room table, eating in silence. True to his word, Thatch ate every bite. Once finished, he helped her carry everything back to the kitchen and even handwashed the dishes before passing her the wet items to dry. It felt normal. Why did it feel so normal to be cooking and washing dishes with this huge, handsome demon?

She glanced at the clock. There was no guessing how long Paisley would be gone. Or even if Paisley would be coming home tonight. The thought burned Aster's cheeks. What would Thatch do if Aster had to stay there by herself the entire night? It wasn't like she'd never slept alone in an empty house before, but not after a fairy had been murdered so close. Not when she had a bodyguard who vowed to be wherever she was.

"Um…what do you want to do now?"

Thatch's gaze appraised her as he leaned against the counter. "Whatever you want to do."

A heat bloomed from her toes and rushed all the way to the roots of her hair. "Movie?"

"Sure."

"Do you have a genre preference? I'm afraid that Paisley's collection consists mostly of rom-coms and animated films."

"I can do a rom-com."

Smiling, she led Thatch into the parlor, where she selected *What Women Want* because she thought Mel Gibson's character and the funny storyline would be a good film to watch with a demon who may not have ever watched a single rom-com in his life. She couldn't get over her disappointment when Thatch chose to sit in a high-backed chair rather than share the couch with her. Yes, it was small, but she wouldn't have minded being close to Thatch on those tiny cushions. Eventually, though, she rested her head on the armrest and actually fell asleep.

A jostling motion pried her awake, and she came to in Thatch's arms. She peered up at him, wondering if he were real. Was he really holding her in his large, muscular arms?

"Where's your bedroom?" His voice was deep, deeper than usual.

Heart racing, she said, "Upstairs. First door on the right."

He carried her away without another word. While he ascended the stairs, she spotted his wide hand gliding up the banister, and she realized he wasn't holding her in both of his arms. He was carrying her one-handed. His arm that should be at her back, supporting her, wasn't there. She quickly slung her arms around his neck, which made him chuckle.

"I'm not going to drop you, baby doll."

At her door, he opened it with his free hand. She expected him to set her on her feet then, but he didn't. Rather, he brought her all the way to her bed. Bending over, he pulled back her white featherdown comforter. Then he set her in the middle of the bed. She felt so tiny in her bed, with him towering over her. All she could do was lay there and gape up at him while he tucked her in. Her heart pounded with such force against her ribcage that she was sure her bed shook beneath her from the beats.

"Why do you do that?"

He braced his fisted hands on either side of her and

leaned down. "Do what?"

"Call me 'baby doll'?"

He tilted his head. "Because you're petite, and all I want to do is carry you around like a child would a baby doll, but if you don't like it, tell me, and I'll stop saying it."

"No." She bolted upright.

He shifted back when her face came within inches of his.

"Please don't stop. I like it."

He lifted his left hand from the mattress and cupped her cheek. "Then goodnight, baby doll."

"Night."

His thumb grazed her cheek up and down. When she thought he might kiss her, he straightened. "I'll see you in the morning."

"Okay. Sweet dreams, Thatch."

"I have a feeling I'll have very sweet dreams tonight." With that, he left her bedroom and shut the door at his back.

Shaken, she huddled down and hugged the comforter to herself. She wasn't sure if she'd ever fall asleep, but she somehow managed it.

In the middle of the night, she cracked open her eyelids and gasped at the sight of a dark shadow on the other side of her curtains. Someone was there. Outside her bedroom. Spying? Hoping to sneak in and kill her in bed?

Shaking now for an all-new reason, she reached for her cell phone. Paisley didn't often carry her cell phone. Should she call Case? Honestly, she didn't want to disturb him or Paisley. But she didn't have Thatch's number. Did Thatch even have a mobile phone? Not many in the Enchanted Hierarchy did. There tended to be a distaste for anything human to make it into their territory, but that didn't stop creatures from smuggling in some goods. After all, they got their TVs, DVDs, and other electronic devices straight from the Un-Enchanted.

No. She wouldn't call Case or Paisley. Whoever was outside her bedroom, she'd get a good look at them and then handle it herself. She had a whole bag of dust that could do significant damage to an intruder. Her bag of fairy dust still hung from her hip. Also on her nightstand was a bag of spikes and blow dart. She could do even more damage with those. So, she plucked them up, slipped out of bed, and tiptoed to the glass door of her balcony.

Holding her breath, she used the tip of her finger to draw back the curtain and peeked out. A stranger wasn't there. Certainly not a killer. It was Thatch, sitting on one of her balcony chairs, with a plush blanket covering his legs. She was about to step back from the window when she noticed something tall protruding from the middle of his lap. In the darkness, she couldn't make out what it was, but she could see his hand wrapped around it. His hand stroked up and down whatever he held. A groan rumbled out of him.

She frowned. Was he okay? Was he hurt?

He groaned again.

She was about to open the door to check on his wellbeing when he hissed, "Aster."

His voice saying her name had her stilling.

"You're so beautiful." His hand moved faster.

What he was doing became startling clear. He was masturbating. While thinking of her.

On the other side of the glass door, she was riveted. She couldn't look away. She knew she should; this was a private moment, an intimate moment, meant only for him that she shouldn't be witnessing, but her eyes were wide, and she couldn't so much as blink, for she didn't want to miss a single second.

His eyes were closed. His other hand made an appearance, and he gripped the base of his dick. There was no mistaking what it was now. And it was massive. With his impressive body, it shouldn't surprise her that he'd have a penis to match, but she didn't really know about those things. She'd never seen one before; she was a virgin, and the visual she had now—of his cock covered by a plush blanket—it gave her butterflies.

"Aster." His hips jutted beneath the blanket. "I want you, Aster. I want you so much."

She was panting behind the door, fogging up the glass with her breath. A throbbing sensation bloomed between her legs. She squirmed. It felt strange. Hands shaking, she carefully swiped the moisture from the glass with her thumb so she could continue to watch him fall apart under his own hands, with her name on his lips, her face on his mind.

He moaned, and his hand quickened. "Aster…Aster." His voice became more urgent. It was as though he were calling for her, and, Goddess, she wanted to go to him. Her body jittered with that knowledge, but if she went to him, she wouldn't know what to do.

What would *he* do?

Staying put, behind that curtain, was the best thing to do. The only thing to do. Don't move. Don't breathe. Don't for one second look away.

So, she didn't.

He was so sexy lounging in that chair, with the blanket hiding his lower half from sight, his eyelids screwed tightly shut, his head tipped back as his hand brought him pleasure. What would it take for her to bring him the same pleasure?

Her mouth went dry at the thought.

Moans left him, and they were sounds unlike any she'd heard before. She'd never heard a man make those noises because of her, not even indirectly.

His hand jerked up and down his length so fast now, aided by the smooth glide of the plush blanket. Seeing that summoned a wet heat between her legs that slithered over her. She clenched her thighs together to stop it, but there was no stopping it now that it had begun.

Thatch lifted his hips off the chair and let out a groan that had her scrambling backward from the glass door. She didn't have to be experienced to understand that he'd finished. Thoughts of her had brought this great demon to orgasm. She had no idea what that felt like, and she yearned to know.

Turned on from what she'd seen, she climbed back into bed. Beneath her comforter, she slipped her panties down her thighs and off her ankles. She let them fall to the floor. Head turned toward the balcony's doors, she could make out Thatch's shadow, knew he was still there, post-orgasm. Biting her bottom lip, fully aware that she was going to engage in something erotic with a demon right outside her bedroom, moments after he himself came because of her, she slid her fingers up the inside of her thighs.

Already, they trembled.

She brought her fingers to her pussy, felt how drenched she was after spying on Thatch. Her vulva was already swollen with arousal. She stroked her wet lips, wondering, wondering what it'd be like if Thatch were paying her attention instead. What would his touch feel like? What would he do? How would he treat her? How would he give her pleasure?

The glide of her fingers felt so good on her aroused flesh. The slickness at her fingertips was marvelous. She'd never been so wet before. There was so much of it that she could fingerpaint with it, create something erotic on a canvas with her cum. Instead of a canvas, she painted her cum over herself.

Looking at Thatch's shadow through the curtains, she did something she only did when she was ovulating, only a few nights a month, and only for six months a year…she slipped a finger inside herself. Her pussy was wetter and hotter than she'd ever felt it before. She glided her finger in and out, marveling over the way her body accepted the invasion. Her finger slid so easily into a part of herself that no one but herself knew. A secret place that she hoped to share one day …with the demon whose shadow she couldn't stop staring at.

She pushed a second finger into her pussy, found she was so aroused, so wet that two fingers could dip deep inside her and not cause any sort of discomfort. From the times she'd self-pleasured, she knew what felt good, so she crooked her fingers, stroking the cushiony, interior walls of her vagina with her fingertips. She brought her other hand between her thighs, seeking more. As she massaged her g-zone, she swirled the creaminess of her arousal over her clit.

Tingles and warmth.

Sensations she'd experienced before intensified.

Sighs became soft moans.

Her hips lifted off the mattress.

Her legs trembled.

Those tingles became sparks.

That warmth became a flood of heat.

The sensations quadrupled.

Overwhelmed from the pleasure, she let her hands still and her body go lax. It was too much. While it felt good, and she desperately wanted to finish, she just couldn't continue. Not even when she was ovulating could she manage to reach climax. She had no idea what it felt like to orgasm, and she badly yearned for one right now. Frustrated, she glanced toward the curtains. Thatch's shadow was still there. The urge to slide open that door and ask him to help her reach completion was tempting. Too tempting. So, she rolled onto her side, putting her back to the curtains, and clutched a pillow between her legs, willing the sensations to fade.

4

Permission

Thatch left at sun-up, showered, dressed in fresh clothes, and returned to Paisley's. He knocked on the front door, not sure if Aster would be awake yet or not, but the door opened, and she stood there in the tiniest dress imaginable. A dress that could easily fit an actual baby doll.

The bodice looked as though it was made from a bra's cups the way that they formed to her breasts and exposed their sensual curves. Pastel-colored flowers along the straps followed the curves of her sides and then looped around her slender waist. A tulle skirt flared around her luscious hips and fell inches shy of her shapely backside. If she bent over, her ass would be on display for all. Good thing she was home, and he'd make sure she stayed home.

For several heartbeats, he couldn't tear his gaze off that little dress, though. So short. He imagined sitting her down on that itty bitty couch, parting her legs, and settling his head between her thighs, beneath those puffy layers of tulle that barely concealed her. He'd listen to her sweet voice cry out while he licked her vulva, which he'd lick and lick until she came on his tongue.

His cock stirred in his pants.

Diablo.

He tore his gaze from the hem and met her eyes. The dress was lavender, identical to the shade of her irises, increasing their alluring power.

So gorgeous.

"Good morning, baby doll."

"Good morning. I didn't know you'd left. Where did you…umm…spend the night?"

"I posted outside your balcony."

"My balcony? All night?"

"That's right."

Her balcony, where he couldn't stop thinking of her in her bed. Warm and soft. He thought of her so much that his cock had hardened. Then he'd thought of her while he stroked himself. And he'd thought of her when he came all over a blanket, as soft and warm as her.

"You didn't know I was out there?"

She shook her head quickly, and her cheeks flushed.

Was the adorable little fairy lying to him? Had she known he was out there? Protecting her? Jerking off to her?

Her gaze lowered, and he grinned when he realized she was staring right at his crotch. *Did you see me last night, baby doll*?

Part of him hoped she did. The other part of him didn't want to harm their bodyguard and principal relationship. And that was the most important thing right now. He had to protect her. So, no more jerking off while he was on duty. No matter how tempting.

But she was still eyeing his crotch.

"Aster?"

Her gaze didn't budge.

"Baby doll?"

She jolted. "Huh?"

He liked that she responded to his nickname for her.

"Sorry. I got lost in thought."

"You were lost in thought while staring at my—"

"Are you hungry?" she blurted out.

He grinned. "Ravenous."

"I'll make breakfast. Would you like to have breakfast with me?"

"I would."

Aster made banana pancakes with a lavender chocolate drizzle that was to die for. They ate them across from each other at the kitchen table, and Thatch cleaned his plate.

"Do you want more?" she asked.

"No, thank you. It was delicious, though." He brought his plate to the sink and washed it. Then he leaned against the counter. "I don't think Paisley is going to be back today. Case's text earlier hinted they'd may be together. All day. Which means I'm going to stay here with you. What would you like to do?"

Her gaze shifted to his crotch.

Oh, don't do that, baby doll. How am I supposed to be the responsible bodyguard if you keep doing that?

Her eyes flicked back up. "I actually planned to go to the faye faction today."

He jolted. "In that?"

She blinked. "In what?"

"That dress? It's way too small."

She glanced down. "Don't be silly."

"It's too small."

"No, it's not."

He stepped closer. "It is."

She shifted, exuding uncomfortableness at his proximity.

"I'm sorry." He quickly stepped back. "I don't mean to make you uncomfortable, but that dress is far too short."

Her hands riffled along the edge of the hem. "I-I can change."

"No." For despite the fact that he didn't want anyone else to see her in such a revealing and beautiful dress, *he* still desired to see *her* in it. "That's not necessary, but I would ask you to wear a cloak or coat or something. Especially when we're flying. I don't need everyone to see…" He let his words trail off.

Her pretty cheeks turned a lovely shade of pink. She'd probably be able to tell him the exact shade, but it didn't matter right then what the color was called. All that mattered was how it increased her beauty.

"What do you plan to do at the faye faction?"

"Assist with the funeral preparations. Paisley put all the plans together before going to dinner last night, but it's not the queen's job to do the prep. I want to help as much as I can."

"I can help, too."

"That's not a demon's job, either."

"That may be so, but I will be there to offer my hand. I can do whatever's needed, whatever's necessary. I can certainly do any heavy lifting."

"You're too kind, Thatch. I…I'll fetch a cloak."

She went upstairs and came back down with a violet cloak that matched her hair folded over her arm. In front of him, she shook it out and went to put it on.

"Allow me, please."

She relinquished the cloak to him, and he had the honor of draping it over her shoulders and knotting it at her collarbone.

Outside, they paused in the grass. "It'd be much quicker if I flew. Do you consent to being carried?"

She nodded, and he swept her up. In his arms, she tucked the cloak around her legs and then snuggled close to his chest. That right there could melt any demon. He didn't care what kind of demon you were. You'd be a puddle of horns from having such a sweet creature cuddle up against you. He had two reactions that betrayed him. One, his heart fluttered in his chest. Two, his dick stirred. If he could, he'd carry her off somewhere private right then and do everything in his power to prove to her that he was worthy of her. Worthy to be with her in a way that fairies and demons shouldn't be, but it was all he desired. All and so much more.

Trying to stay his urges, he launched into the air.

Perfumed tendrils of her hair slithered around his neck, tickling and enticing him with their feel and scent.

Moments later, they arrived at the faye faction.

Aster pointed him to the main house in the center of the flowering town where important fairy matters took place. He landed on a cobblestone walkway. Nearby fairies jumped as if he were about to attack them. Never mind the fact that he had no way to cause anyone harm while holding a fairy in his arms. He glanced down at Aster, a fairy who seemed completely happy to be right there in his arms. Wishful thinking, perhaps, but he'd continue to think it.

He set Aster gently to her feet, and she untied the knot at her throat. "I'll hold onto that for you, baby doll."

"Thank you." She handed him her cloak.

He laid it over his arm and held it to his middle. His gaze drifted over to the fairies nearby who were either gawking at him or shivering with fear.

"Don't worry about them. They'll see you don't mean them any harm."

And then she did something that would scandalize the entire Enchanted Hierarchy. She took his hand and led him right into the main house. The moment they stepped inside, everyone turned to look, and when they saw him, silence loomed.

A fairy with hair the color of pumpkins hustled over. "Aster, dear. W-who is your escort?"

"This is Thatch. He's my friend."

"Bodyguard," he corrected.

"Friend slash bodyguard. Thatch, this is my aunt, Chrysanthemum."

"Oh, please, it's just Mum. How do you do, Thatch?"

He bowed slightly at the waist, unsure of how to answer that. He wasn't accustomed to such formal talk.

"How long will you be with us?" Mum asked.

"As long as Aster is here, I'll be here, too."

"Splendid. Make yourself at home."

He inclined his head.

"Come on, Thatch." Aster took his hand again and pulled him over to a table where a few other fairies worked. White flower petals dusted the surface. "We're making garlands of white daisies that will form a circle, a fairy ring, around the hole in the ground where Dahlia will be laid to rest. I can show you how it's done."

He paid attention to Aster's instructions and mimicked them the best he could, but his large demon hands and fingers weren't so skilled in twining flower stems and greenery into a lovely rope. Still, he did his best and continued to make attempts, even when Aster had to sweetly fix what he'd done. The whole time, he sensed all the fairies in the room stealing peeks, whispering, and openly gawking.

A fairy had been murdered following the coronation of their queen. For all they knew, ademon was the cause of their beloved fairy's death. And here he was, a demon, joining in on the funeral preparations. Did they think he was there to make a mockery of their traditions? Because he meant no such thing.

He glanced around the room. In the far corner, a group was creating a wicker coffin. The thing looked big enough for a demon child. His gaze lowered to Aster, and his throat tightened like someone was attempting to strangle him, because he realized that she could fit inside that tiny wicker coffin.

In the center of the room, four fairies were sewing at the four corners of a cloth…the fairy's burial cloth. Aster's soft voice came to him, explaining what he saw. "It's biodegradable cloth made from bamboo. They're stitching faye symbols into it to bless Dahlia's soul on the journey to the Summerlands."

"Hasn't her soul already journeyed to the Summerlands?"

She smiled. "We believe she's still here, twined with nature, until we can perform her rites and she can move on in peace."

Demons didn't have such beliefs, but he liked the faye way.

His gaze continued to search the room. In the opposite corner of the creation of the wicker coffin stood a small oak piano, the wood worn down.

With all the fairies there so clearly uneasy with his presence, there was only one thing he could think of doing. He laid down the rope he'd been failing to braid and walked silently over to the piano. When he sat on the bench, it creaked under his weight, but it held. He ran his fingers over the cool keys. It'd been ages since he'd last played. He didn't know how well his fingers would respond as he lowered the keys, letting the first notes sing. It was a simple, sweet song his grandmother had taught him resurrected from his childhood memories, and he played it like it was second nature, hoping that it'd calm the fairies' nerves.

When he finished the song, he brought his hands to his lap and sat there, unsure if he should continue playing or look to see if his playing had had the desired effect on the fairies.

A small hand touched his elbow and slid to his wrist.

He closed his eyes.

Her touch. He could be undone by her touch on his arm alone.

He shifted to the end of the bench, opening up a space for her to sit if she wanted to, but he didn't have the courage to ask. Fortunately, he didn't have to. She took the place he offered without a word. Her hip pressed against his. That little dress of hers came to the top of her thigh, just shy of a place he desired to explore. Diablo, he should've asked her to change.

"You play beautifully."

"Thank you. Not many would believe a demon's hands could create music."

"Why not?"

"Because a demon's hands are believed to only cause pain."

"That can't be true. If it were, Paisley wouldn't be with Case. It seems his hands don't cause her pain."

Thatch snorted. "Yeah, well, he's a sex demon."

"Oh." There her cheeks went again, coloring with a lovely blush. "Well, I don't think it's true that a demon's hands can only cause pain. You've held me several times in your arms, and held my hand, and you didn't cause me an ounce of pain." She took his right hand now in hers. "In fact, your hands are beautiful."

"No, they're not."

"Yes, they are." She studied his hand. "Your hands are strong and beautiful and summon sweet music right at the tips. I have a feeling that they can do more than that."

"They could. With permission."

She bent her head toward his hand. Her breath warmed his fingers. Her lips brushed his skin. Then she reached for his other hand and bent her head over it, too. Breath. Lips. His own breath catching. His own lips parting.

The next thing he knew, she was getting up.

He turned on the bench. "What was that?"

She met his eye. "I was giving them permission."

5

Daisy Chains

Thatch continued to play songs while Aster helped finish up the fairy ring and then pitched in with making daisy chains that every fairy in attendance would wear. She couldn't stop from looking at Thatch. He sat at the piano, playing song after song, as if his sole goal was to keep the fairies' minds occupied while they worked.

When he first sat at the piano, he'd captivated her. Such a large demon creating a song of faye origin. The fact he knew it was not only strange but curious. Still, he played it with such skill that he'd mesmerized all the fairies there. Her heart had fluttered at the sight of him. It fluttered again now as she gazed at him, the daisy chain she'd been crafting forgotten.

Mum nudged her, and she resumed her task.

Tomorrow, the ceremony would take place. She'd be in attendance, which meant Thatch would be there, too. The last thing she wanted was for the other fairies to be uncomfortable with him there. She wanted them, and him, to know he was welcome, so she set about braiding a special daisy chain just for him. Once she finished, she hid the daisy chain in her satchel to give to him later.

Mum tapped her arm. "His playing is beautiful, but I think we have a chore for him that would greatly help us. If he's willing, of course. It'd cut down on time."

"What is it?"

"Dahlia's grave needs to be dug.

"I'll ask." She went to him and stepped beside him again.

He stopped playing.

"We have a favor to ask of you, if you're willing."

He rotated on the bench. "Whatever you need."

"The hole for Dahlia's wicker coffin needs to be dug. Would you mind?"

"Not at all."

He accepted the shovel Mum had for him and followed Aster into the forest where Dahlia's body would be laid to rest between two great maple trees.

"Right here."

He rolled up his sleeves and went straight to work, plunging the shovel into the earth. One scoop at a time, he removed clumps of earth. He didn't just dig a hole to get the job done but made the sides perfectly symmetrical and the corners even. Aster couldn't help but watch him while she went about tidying the area of weeds and fallen branches, and placing rosemary around to deter ants from bugging guests during the ceremony.

She had a feeling she knew exactly what Paisley had felt when she'd seen Case working with the earth to fix the daemon faction brand someone had burned into the grass, because Thatch, with dirt smeared on his forearms and hands, was a vision. He was more than handsome. He was sexy. Shovel in hand. Dirt in the creases of his knuckles.

So incredibly, demonically sexy.

"Is this good?"

Aster bit her bottom lip. *Very good.*

"Aster?"

She was thinking about what she'd whispered to his hands. *I give you permission to bring me pleasure that I've never felt before.*

"Baby doll?"

She blinked. "Huh?"

"Is this good? I think it's deep enough."

She studied the carefully dug grave. "It's perfect. You did great, Thatch."

"It's the least I could do."

"You did a lot of good here today, Thatch. It won't be forgotten."

They returned to the main house to relinquish the shovel. On the cobblestone walkway, Aster fixed the cloak around her shoulders.

Thatch lifted his hands. "I'm covered in dirt now."

"I'm a fairy. I'm not afraid of dirt."

"If you're sure."

She stepped up to him. "I'm sure."

He lifted her into his arms and flew back to Paisley's. "I'll need to go to Case's to shower."

"You can shower here."

"I don't have any clothes here."

"You should maybe bring some…if Paisley continues to stay there, you won't want to walk in and find them going at it on the staircase."

He grimaced. "Diablo."

She giggled. "And if you're serious about continuing to be my bodyguard—"

"I've never been more serious."

His reply sent flutters through her. "In that case, pun not intended, I'm always here, so it'd make sense for you to stay here, too. There's a guest bedroom on the first floor. I can show it to you."

He considered her a moment before saying, "Alright, but I do need to go back to get clothes, and I don't want to leave you here."

"I can come with you. If we walk in on something, you can cover my eyes."

"Then who will cover mine?"

She laughed. "Pick me up with one arm, cover my eyes with the other, and then I can cover yours."

"Sounds like a plan." He picked her up with one arm right then.

He didn't put her down even when they got to Case's. She wondered if he had any idea how hot it was that he carried her all the way to his room, without a word, and set her right on his bed. He still didn't say anything when he opened a walk-in closet. The sound of hangers sliding met her ears. When he came back out, he held a full duffel bag. He was a quick packer, that was for sure.

"Alright, baby doll, stand up on my bed."

She blinked. "What?"

"Climb up so I can pick you up."

"Oh, right." She scrambled onto his bed and stood, bringing herself face to face with him. Staring into his eyes, she looped her arms around his shoulders, and he hooked his free arm behind her, just below her ass. He drew her to him so that she was flat against his chest.

"Ready?"

"Mm-hm."

He kept her tucked close the entire time he flew her home. Once inside, he set her feet on the tile. "Where's the guest bathroom?"

She pointed. "Right hall. First door on the left. And the guest bedroom is right across from it."

"I'm going to take a fast shower and change. Stay inside. Please."

"I will. I promise."

He went off to clean up, and she went to the kitchen to make them something to eat. She'd just finished compiling sandwiches when Thatch stepped into the kitchen in fresh clothes. Goddess, he looked good in fitted pants and button-up shirts. So good.

"Here. I made you a Green Goddess Sandwich." Suddenly conscious that she made a demon a veggie sandwich, she passed him a plate. "Um. Do you like avocados?"

"I do."

"Cucumbers?"

"Yeah."

"Lettuce?"

"Nothing wrong with it."

"Do you care if your sandwich doesn't have any meat?"

"I can eat a veggie sandwich." He accepted the plate. "Thank you, baby doll."

They ate the sandwiches side by side.

"Um…is the guestroom okay?"

"Bed is a little small."

She scanned him from horns to feet. "Right. If you don't like that bed, you can sleep anywhere you want to."

"Anywhere?" His voice was a deep growl that sent a thrill of awareness through her entire body.

"A-anywhere."

He grinned real slow. "The bed in the guestroom is fine. For now."

That 'for now' sped up her heartrate.

"Um…I'm off to bed. The funeral is at sunrise."

"Sleep well, baby doll."

"You too."

As she went upstairs, she wondered if he'd masturbate again tonight knowing she was just upstairs, in a bed she'd practically offered to him.

Before the sun's rays speared over the horizon, Aster dressed in a white sundress and found Thatch waiting for her. She pulled the daisy chain she made for him out of her satchel. "Here. Everyone at the ceremony will be wearing one."

He took the daisy chain. "You made this for me?"

"Yeah. I didn't want you to feel left out…and…" She peered at her feet. "I don't know…I wanted to do something for you." He was still staring at it, making her nervous that he hated it or thought it was ridiculous. "But if you don't want to wear it then—" She went to take it back, but he lifted it out of reach.

"When did you hear me say I wouldn't wear it?"

"I thought…"

"You made it for me because you were being thoughtful, and I will wear it." To prove it, he slipped the daisy chain over his horns, settled it into place around his neck, and pulled his braid free. "Thank you, baby doll, for thinking of me."

"Of…of course."

He reached out and stroked his thumb and index finger down a lock of her hair. "You look beautiful."

"So do you."

He smiled. "Ready to go?"

"I am."

He picked her up.

"You don't have to carry me everywhere we go."

"I fly faster than you."

"You're so sure about that?"

He grinned. "You want to race, baby doll?"

"Maybe. Are you scared you'll lose to a fairy?"

"When it's safe, you're on, but in the meantime, I'll carry you wherever we go."

She laid a hand to the middle of his chest. "I can deal with that."

They met Paisley in the forest at the ceremony site. Thatch stood on the outskirts to make his presence as lowkey as possible, although it was impossible not to notice him, sense him.

Paisley said a few words before four fairies made a magickal circle by calling on the four elements and the four fairy guardians in each direction. Once that was completed, a faye high priestess performed the ritual and led prayers. After the final prayer and song was sung, fairies lowered the wicker coffin containing Dahlia into the hole Thatch had dug.

As everyone left, they tossed a white rose into the hole, covering the wicker coffin so nothing but white petals and green leaves were visible.

Thatch tossed in the last rose, earning the respect of every fairy there. And the fact he wore a daisy chain hadn't gone unnoticed, either. Even though he was a demon, what he had done for the faye faction and Dahlia was known by every fairy.

When he picked Aster up, a few fairies swooned.

Sure, there may be an unspoken rule that creatures not intermingle and procreate, but fairies revered nature and love and saw nothing wrong with two different creatures being together. Fairies were the most open-minded and accepting of creatures in all the Enchanted Hierarchy, followed by elves. So, it was no surprise that Thatch could make her, or other fairies, swoon. She was just thankful that he was her bodyguard and no one else's.

Over the next two weeks, they cooked and baked, gardened and took walks, watched rom-coms and visited the faye faction, where he was rapidly becoming a part of the faye community. She missed Paisley, though, so when Paisley asked her if she wanted to have a spa day and a girls' night, she couldn't contain her happiness.

Sitting in a sauna with cotton towels wrapped around them, Aster and Paisley caught up, which meant they spent fifteen minutes talking about Case. With their muscles warm and relaxed, they stretched out for full-body massages that had Aster giggling because she was ticklish. Now, lying in the coziest chairs ever, with all-natural masks hardening on their faces, Pasiley changed the topic of discussion from Case to Thatch.

"So, how has it been with Thatch?"

"It's been good. Nice. He's sweet…and I like to be around him…with him."

"Mm-hm. I've heard he's been making waves at the faye faction."

"What do you mean?"

"Mum was gushing about him at the ceremony, and when she said his name, a few fairies behind her almost swooned right to the ground."

"I've noticed that, too."

"Uh-huh. Are the two of you more than bodyguard and principal?"

"Principal?" Her eyes widened. "Wait. Do you think that's the only way he thinks of me? As his principal?"

"Aster, I think he's head over horns for you."

Thank Goddess for the mask hiding her blush. She cleared her throat. "No, w-we are not more than bodyguard and principal, but"—her face was so hot she worried the mask would melt off—"I'd like him to be more than just my bodyguard. I want him to be my boyfriend." She frowned. "Is boyfriend too weird for a demon? Maybe he can be my demonfriend?"

"Demonfriend, boyfriend, I think it's a real possibility."

"Really?"

"Really, really."

Following a nice gossip session, they got their nails, hair, and makeup done. When they finished, they found Thatch stuffed into a small chair in the waiting room and a roomful of fairies batting their lashes in his direction. He didn't seem to notice them, or at least was ignoring them while he flipped the page in a book.

When they stepped out, he set the book on the coffee table and got to his feet. The second he stood, the fairies sighed in unison.

Yeah, he was a sight to behold. All that height. Those wide shoulders. That long, silky braid. His lean hips. He was a top-notch demon. But he wasn't hers. That fact ruined the good mood she was in from the pampering.

He's not mine. Not really.

6

The Midnight Lair

T

Thatch noticed the shift in Aster's mood instantly. "What's wrong?"

She didn't meet his eye. "Nothing."

"Don't lie to me, baby doll. What's wrong?"

She glanced at Paisley. "Nothing. I promise."

He peered at Paisley, too, who shrugged.

The two of them walked ahead of him back to Paisley's. The whole way, he wondered about why her mood had changed and admired the way her hips moved, how the skirt of her dress swished over her shapely behind, and how her hair blew in the breeze. He wished they had a longer walk, but in a short time, they arrived at Paisley's house that now felt like his own home.

The past two weeks with Aster in that house had been fun. They weren't supposed to be having fun; he was there to do a job, but with no threats and no danger, they'd been able to bond. He just wished he could bond some more with her. Intimately. Except, he wasn't sure if he could be intimate with her. His anatomy was large, and she was petite. He'd never want to hurt her, so it might not ever be possible. This dream. This fantasy.

Aster and Paisley planned to watch a movie, safely indoors, and since he was barred from the house for the next two hours, he intended to go to Case's to check in with the other members of Case's council. He was hesitant to leave, though. He hadn't left Aster for longer than a few minutes, other than when she slept upstairs and when he slept downstairs. Even so, he barely slept. Both from being on high alert and from thinking about her.

"Thatch, Aster and I can keep each other safe while you're gone," Paisley said. "Just ask Case about how good she is with a blow dart. We'll be fine. We'll just be watching *Spice World*, a masterpiece of a movie—I don't care what anyone says—and eating loads of candy."

He glanced at Aster. "Alright. Just please, both of you, stay inside."

"We will." Aster plopped onto the love seat. "We'll be right here."

"Okay." Still, he was reluctant, even while pulling the door shut behind him and waiting to hear Paisley lock it from the inside.

The locks tumbled, and he took off.

He met with Case, and they called a council meeting to get an update on the efforts to uncover who had murdered an innocent fairy who had done nothing wrong but be easy prey for the bastards wanting to scare Paisley. Paisley didn't seem like one to be so easily scared, though, which meant they'd do more to get her attention. They'd do something that would horrify her. Or target someone who would put fear into her. And that would be Aster.

He shifted in his seat to the right of Case, because he shouldn't be there. Paisley and Aster were alone in a house that someone had gotten close to twice already. Once, to leave behind thousands of beheaded bats on the day of Paisley's coronation and then again to place severed fairy wings in her yard.

Case glanced at him.

Thatch met his eye.

"We can't let these fuckers get another chance to do something else. Thatch is guarding Aster, and I'm with Paisley as much as possible, but we can't do this forever."

Wrong. Thatch would be Aster's bodyguard for the rest of his life.

"No matter how much I enjoy my time with Paisley, she's too independent to allow me to keep her caged up like this, even with sex involved."

Thatch grumbled. "We *don't* want to hear about that."

"Speak for yourself," someone said.

"My point is," Case continued, "this isn't a long-term plan. We have to find the culprits. When we do, I have a cell just for them in my dungeon and a list of ways I intend to bring them pain. They'll be permanent residents."

Thatch nodded, liking that idea very much.

"The next time I call a meeting, we better have something concrete, and not a whole lot of nothing like we've been having." Case stood. "Dismissed."

They all got to their feet and left.

Thatch followed Case to the parlor. "No plans with Paisley tonight?"

"Nope. Paisley and Aster have decided to extend it to a girls' night, which you should know as Aster's bodyguard."

He knew very well that Paisley and Case didn't have any plans, because girls' night was still in full swing. Aster and Paisley would be leaving at any moment to go to The Midnight Lair. He'd wanted to escort them, but they were going to fly to get there faster, and Paisley wouldn't let him catch a glimpse of her wings. So, he'd been instructed to meet them at the club to continue his protector duties.

Had Paisley shown Case her wings at least? He understood her not wanting to show him; he wasn't anything to her. Not really.

Thatch sat on the love seat while Case went to a bottle of whiskey and a clean highball glass. "You didn't ask Paisley what their plans were?"

The sound of whiskey splashing into a glass met Thatch's ears.

"It's none of my business what they do during girls' time."

Interesting. Did Case not know what they'd done so far? Did he not know they were going clubbing tonight? "So, you don't know what they did today?"

"I do not."

Well, this'll be fun. "They spent the day at The Faye Time Spa. A sauna and full-body massages were on the agenda."

"Relaxing."

Thatch smirked at Case's back, well aware that Case was feeling the first inklings of curiosity and jealousy. "Followed by facials and getting their nails, hair, and makeup done."

"Sounds like a complete spa day."

"Indeed, and tonight they're planning to dance and have drinks." Thatch knew very well the thought of Paisley dancing and having drinks would get to Case.

"Girls' night wouldn't be girls' night without dancing and a couple of drinks."

Thatch spoke the words that would change Case's tune. "At the club that opened recently…The Midnight Lair."

Case's spine shifted even straighter. Tension pulled his shoulders back.

"I told Aster I will go to the club with them, to protect her, even during girls' night."

"As I would expect you to."

"Well—" Thatch stood. "They plan to get to the club by ten."

Case glanced at the grandfather clock. "You better hurry."

"My priority is Aster, but I'll keep an eye on Paisley, too. It shouldn't be too hard if they stick together." He intended to make sure no one came near them or touched them. If they did, there'd be severe consequences.

"You're going to a club, Thatch. Have a little fun and dance with the cute fairy."

Thatch flinched. "I couldn't do that."

"Yes, you could. Have a little liquid courage and dance with Aster."

Thatch didn't drink, but the urge to dance with Aster, to feel her close, was fierce. But still…he couldn't.

"Consider that an order."

Shoot. Even a silly order like that he wouldn't be able to ignore.

"Now go. Get there before they do."

Thatch nodded. "I'll contact you if anything happens."

"Appreciate it."

Bass pumping.

Bodies humping.

Drinks spilling.

The Midnight Lair was packed with creatures looking to have fun and demons looking to have sex, and Aster and Paisley were in the center of it. Paisley wore a black ensemble that would drive Case up the wall with lust. Dancing in front of her, looking radiant in a pink dress that flowed from her hips to her knees, was Aster. Her hair was pinned up, exposing the lovely length of her neck and her sweet collarbones. The bodice of her dress framed her luscious breasts. Diablo, she was a treat in that dress, on that dance floor, and all the demons and horny creatures there seemed to agree. They were circling around Aster and Paisley like bloodthirsty hellhounds.

Thatch wedged his way through the crowd.

Aster saw him approaching as she danced. Her eyes lit up. "Thatch!"

Paisley turned. "Thatch, when a girl is that happy to see you, you're obligated to dance with her. I'll allow one dance during girls' night."

Diablo. What the hell were Case and Paisley doing to him?

He peered at Aster as she gazed up at him expectantly. "I'm sorry, baby doll, but I don't dance. I'd just step on your feet. Hurt you."

"Not if I *stood* on your feet."

"I still wouldn't know what to do. I can waltz, but I can't dance to this."

"That's okay, Thatch." She took his hand. "We don't ever have to fast dance."

He skimmed his thumb over her knuckles. "I'll let the two of you get back to your fun. I'll be at the bar, keeping an eye on you both."

"Try to have a little fun," Paisley said.

He groaned. "You and Case are too much alike sometimes."

"I'm choosing to take that as a compliment."

Thatch smirked. "Excuse me." He turned his gaze to Aster. "I'll be right over there if you need me."

"Okay."

He extracted his fingers from hers, although he

didn't want to release her. Then he made his way to the bar.

A demon bartender came over. "What would you like to drink?"

"Sparkling water. No ice. Lemon."

The bartender cracked open a fresh bottle of sparkling water and added a slice of lemon to the glass. He placed the drink on a napkin and pushed it toward Thatch.

"Thank you." Thatch picked up the glass and leaned his back against the bar so he could watch Aster and Paisley. He had no more than turned when he spied a slimy incubus moving in behind Paisley with a clear motive in mind. If the gleam of lust in his eyes wasn't enough proof, then the boner pointing at Paisley's ass certainly was. "You've got to be kidding me." Thatch slammed his glass down and took a step.

Aster took Paisley's hands and spun her around, taking Paisley's spot. The incubus was directly behind her when she swung a wing back, slapping the incubus so hard that he toppled to the floor. Still dancing, she took a step back, and stomped her pink heel with perfect aim onto the incubus' crotch. Immediately afterward, Aster hopped around and feigned innocence.

Even from there he could read her lips. "Oh my Goddess." She folded her hands to her chest. "I'm so sorry. I didn't see you there. Are you okay?"

Face red, tears streaming down his face, the incubus struggled to get to his feet.

"Would you like me to get help?"

The incubus waved her off and hobbled away, cupping his package in his hands. That limp indicated serious damage had been done by Aster's tiny foot.

The moment he was gone, Aster twirled to Paisley, who grabbed her as they collapsed into hysterics.

"Diablo, did that little fairy just castrate him with a pink high heel?"

Thatch glanced back at the bartender with a grin. "I think she might have."

"Damn."

Aster slapped an orc with her wing who'd been inching up behind her, clearly not having gotten the message when she'd crippled an incubus seconds ago.

The orc staggered back as if startled. He wisely changed direction.

"She's feisty." The bartender chuckled.

"She is, indeed." Amused, Thatch propped his elbows on the bar top and enjoyed the show as Aster and Paisley shooed demon after demon away from each other with clever maneuvers and a few choice words that Thatch couldn't hear. As they took care of each other out there on the dancefloor, he became mesmerized by Aster. The way she moved. The smile on her face. She was simply gorgeous. He couldn't tear his gaze away.

When Case showed up, he wasn't surprised in the least, but he did laugh. "I had a feeling you'd come."

"I thought it would be nice to have a drink out. That's all."

"Sure."

Aster and Paisley danced together, not for show, not for anyone watching, imagining, fantasizing, just for each other, for fun. That didn't stop patrons from attempting to get in on the action, to steal a piece that wasn't theirs. A demon reached toward Aster's shoulder, as if to force her around.

Case growled and jerked forward.

Thatch blocked Case with his arm, preventing him from storming onto that dancefloor and snapping a demon's forearm. Just as Thatch knew they would, Aster and Paisley took care of it themselves. Paisley wrenched the demon's hand off Aster the second it made contact and hissed at him in such a way that the demon scurried away with his tail between his legs.

"They've been scaring demons off each other since they got here," Thatch said. "You should've seen the wing slap Aster gave an incubus when he moved in on Paisley. It knocked him on his ass, and then Aster stomped her dainty foot right on his crotch. She apologized innocently while the demon slunk off holding his junk."

Case grinned like a proud big brother. "I wish I'd seen that."

"Yeah, turns out I'm not really needed."

They watched them dance. That demon, and all the ones before him, hadn't lessened Aster and Pasiley's mood or changed a thing. They were still having fun, and Thatch loved to see that. He especially enjoyed seeing Aster with her eyes twinkling and laughter floating from her pretty pink lips.

"I'm going to let Paisley know I'm here," Case said, interrupting Thatch's meditation on Aster's beauty. "I'm not going to hide it, but I'll be back. Girls' night is still in full swing."

Thatch snorted. Girls' night was going to end with either Paisley sneaking off to be with Case, or Case breaking into Paisley's to steal her away from girls' night. With the way the two of them had been going lately, dang-near inseparable, it was bound to happen. He stood back a moment before joining them. As he approached, he heard Aster say, "I did *not* dislocate his shoulder."

Case's voice rang with humor. "You don't disagree about crushing his balls, though?"

"Oh, no, I did that." And still she sounded entirely sweet while saying it.

Thatch smirked. "Can we get you ladies something to drink?"

"Long Island Iced Tea," Paisley said.

Aster turned her lovely lavender gaze up to him. "Water for me."

"She's a lightweight," Paisley said.

Case jabbed a thumb in Thatch's direction. "So is he."

Thatch looked up at the ceiling. Have any kind of morals and you were a joke as a demon. "I'm not a lightweight. I don't drink. There's a difference."

"Come on, Thatch." Aster took his hand. "We can be lightweights together."

Okay, so being called a lightweight wasn't so bad after all. Not if it meant he had an adorable fairy to drink sparkling water with.

She tugged on his hand. "We'll get the drinks." And led him to the bar.

"One Long Island Iced Tea, one whiskey neat, and two sparkling waters. Lemon in one and—" He looked to Aster.

"A cherry in the other, please."

The bartender nodded and set to work on getting their drinks ready.

For the first time tonight, they were relatively alone.

Thatch inched closer and caught her intoxicating scent. No wonder why the demons there were being drawn to her like a moth to a flame. Her scent, made stronger by her happiness from dancing, was attracting them. "You look beautiful."

"Thank you."

"I wish you didn't look so beautiful."

She blinked. "What do you mean?"

"I mean, with how beautiful you look and the majestic perfume you're emitting, it's drawing every demon to you. If you and Paisley weren't so good at fending them off yourselves, I would've broken several hands."

"The only demon I want drawn to me is already in front of me."

Thatch stared into her eyes, feeling lost in them, as if they were lavender fields, and inhaled deeply, filling his lungs with that luxurious scent. He opened his mouth, although he had no clue what to say, but the bartender set their drinks down in a neat row on the bar top.

Aster picked up her drink and the whiskey glass.

Thatch picked up his and Paisley's drink.

The two of them made their way back onto the dance floor, where Paisley had her leg around Case in a purely sexual way and Case had his hand up her skirt.

Thatch cleared his throat to get their attention.

Case looked over Paisley's head and grinned. Then

he extracted his hand from a place Thatch didn't want to think about.

Aster held out the whiskey glass to Case.

"Thanks, cutie pie."

Aster beamed with eyes that gleamed. "Thatch ordered it for you."

Case directed his infuriating little smirk to Thatch. "Thanks, cutie pie."

He scowled and grumbled, "I'm not a cutie pie."

The sound of Aster giggling, though, could get him to succumb to being called 'cutie pie' and any number of pet names.

A moment later, the girls shoed them off the dance floor so they could continue having fun without the demon lord and bodyguard there to take up valuable dancing space. They retreated to the bar. Thatch couldn't tear his gaze off Aster. She moved with a provocative grace that stole his breath and kicked his heart rate up a notch or two. There she was: such a sweet, petite fairy dancing with an innocent sensuality to a pop song, and there he was: a demon who was supposed to be a hard shell, only after debauchery, melting like damn butter in the summer heat. It shouldn't be this way, but he didn't care.

Case erupting into laughter drew his attention. "What?"

"We're both so fucking gone that it's not even funny."

Thatch raised a brow. "And yet you're laughing."

Case nodded once while watching Paisley dance. "And yet I'm laughing."

Thatch didn't disagree; he was gone for Aster and

completely fine with. The problem was, he didn't have the faintest clue what to do next. Case was new to relationships, too, but maybe he had an idea. "What do we do about it?"

"You?" Case met his eye. "You go tell Aster that she's the most adorable creature you've ever seen and are utterly fond of her. And then you enjoy whatever happens next. Me?" He turned his attention back to Paisley. "I hang on for the ride and hope I don't lose everything."

The demon lord afraid of losing everything? Had Hell just frozen over?

Thatch was picking up his sparkling water when he heard a demon say something that set his blood on fire. "Diablo, I'd give anything to rail her against one of those speakers."

His gaze ticked to Paisley, who danced right in front of a speaker. He set the glass down with deliberate care, or else it would've shattered in his hand.

"I don't care if she is a hybrid. She looks like she could take a good fucking and dish one out."

Case launched off the bar stool he'd been occupying.

Thatch grabbed him. If Case reached the incubus, there'd be a dead demon on the floor in less than five seconds. Frankly, Thatch didn't care if the incubus lost his life. It was his job, though, to keep the demon lord safe, even if it meant preventing him from murdering a demon who deserved it.

"Well, you can have the queen all you want. I'll take the little fairy."

He jerked toward the demon who'd spoken.

Nothing.

There was absolutely nothing in Thatch's mind but rage.

Nothing.

Absolutely nothing that he yearned to do more than to snap a spine.

Case blocked Thatch with his arm, now halting *him* from taking action.

"She's so damn small. I could pick her up, fuck her like a rag doll, and come inside her until my seed spills out of her and gushes down her legs."

Wrath blinded Thatch with blood-red vision.

A buzzing sound stole his hearing.

Case was no longer holding him back.

"Go for it," the incubus said. "While you do that, I'm going to get the queen to bend the knee for me and worship my cock with her mouth."

No way in Hell would Thatch stop Case from killing the bastard now. He also released Case.

"That's *my* queen you're talking about," Case said.

Thatch stepped behind the demon who had said such disgusting things about Aster. "And that's *my* fairy."

There. He'd said it. He'd claimed his desires. Aster was his. In every way that mattered. She didn't know it, but she had him. She had him, and he didn't want it to be any other way.

The incubus faced them and sneered at Case. The gall. To sneer at the demon lord? He deserved to have that sneering face caved in with a fist. "Afraid she'll like my cock more, *Lord* Case?"

"No, but you should be afraid of losing yours."

Thatch's gaze ticked over to the other demon, the one who he personally wanted to castrate. "You both should." He stood there, listening to the incubus egg Case on and say vile and degrading things about Paisley, a queen, for Diablo's sake. That was another nail in the bastard's coffin. The final nail was the fact that she was Case's woman, Aster's best friend, and Thatch's principal when Case wasn't close. He couldn't let the slimy incubus get away with the things he was saying to Case, about Paisley. "Talking to your lord in that way is a death sentence. If you want to keep your life, you should walk away now."

The other demon tugged the incubus back. "Let's go. It's not worth it."

Wise.

The incubus, though, had to get another jab in. "Enjoy her while you have her."

Admiring Case's restraint, Thatch shoved a whiskey glass at Case. "Drink."

Case downed the drink in one swallow. He probably needed the bottle. "Are you sure you don't want something stronger than sparkling water?"

Thatch swirled the lemon slice around inside his glass. "I'm sure."

They fell into silence while watching Aster and Paisley dance, unaware of what had just gone down. The two were clearly having fun, even after fending off advances the entire time. Paisley danced with a sensuality that could only be a result of being half-vampire, half-fairy, and Aster danced with a clear joy and freedom that brought a smile to Thatch's lips.

"You should've ripped out that demon's spine,"

Case said.

"I was tempted." He stiffened when he spotted another demon working his way toward Aster and Paisley.

"I'm going to make it perfectly clear to every demon in the faction that Paisley and dear, sweet Aster are off limits."

This won't be good.

Then the demon grabbed Paisley.

Definitely not good.

Case tore through the crowd to get to her.

Thatch was right behind him.

Aster's voice, shouting over the music, sounded frantic and fearful. "Hey, let her go!"

Thatch secured an arm around Aster to pull her away from the demon aggressively forcing Paisley to dance with him. Aster's hands instantly latched onto his forearm, and he pulled her backward a step so that her back was flat to him. Her wings beat against him softly. He cupped her shoulders, ran his hands along her arms to calm her nerves and settle her wings, and his touch seemed to do the trick.

Case scared off the demon and snatched up Paisley.

Thatch couldn't hear the words that passed between them, but it was clear the atmosphere had changed. Suddenly, Paisley smacked Case's hand and rammed her shoulder into him while rushing past. She very clearly wanted to get away from him, but it wasn't safe for her to be alone.

Aster realized that at the same time and whacked Case with the back of her hand. "You idiot."

"I know. I—"

"You can't let her fly home alone," Aster said. "Someone with wings tried to shoot her. If they're following her, they'll get their chance."

"She's right," Thatch said. "You need to go after her."

Case met his eye. "Stay with Aster."

Thatch's hands tightened gently on her shoulders. "She won't be without me."

Her wings beat against him again.

When Case smirked, Thatch glared.

Aster reached up and smacked Case again. "Go!"

"See you two later."

They stood in the middle of the dance floor as Case ran after Paisley.

Thatch shifted toward Aster. She looked so beautiful in her pink dress that flowed down her curves in such a pretty way that it had his palms sweating and his heart pounding. The demon's vile and degrading words about what he wanted to do to Aster slammed back to Thatch's mind. He glanced around to see several demons eyeing her and licking their chops. "Do you want to leave?"

"I do, but maybe we can walk, to give them time alone. Would you mind?"

"Would I mind walking with you?" He shook his head. "No, I wouldn't mind walking home with you, baby doll." He took her hand to lead her out of the club. Once out in the fresh air and the silence of the night, he slowed his tread. Neither of them said anything for a while, but Thatch's heart raced. "Are you okay? After everything that happened in there? Are you okay?"

"I'm okay. Because of you."

“I’m not sure how much you really need me. You were beating back demons with a swat of your wings.”

“That’s not true. I need you, Thatch. I really need you.”

He halted and faced her. “Baby doll.” His voice gave out. He didn’t know what to say to that.

She shrugged a shoulder. “I’m just being honest, Thatch.”

He nodded.

She continued walking again, leading him now by the hand. Once more, they fell into silence. After a moment, she pulled her hand free of his and plucked the pins from her hair. The breeze instantly ran its invisible fingers through her locks, and he was instantly jealous, because the wind was doing exactly what he yearned to do himself.

When they reached Paisley’s house, Thatch knew he’d blown this time alone with her.

She and Paisley were going to continue girls’ night there, without him in residence. He only had the next moment left, and he had to know something.

On the doorstep, he laid a hand on Aster’s shoulder. “Baby doll, I need you to answer a question for me.”

“Sure. What is it?”

“When you left the spa, your mood had changed drastically. What happened?”

She gazed at her feet. “All the fairies were staring at you, and…I didn’t like it.”

“How were they staring at me?”

“Not like they were scared.”

“Then how?”

"Like they were lusting after you."

"Well, there's only one fairy whom *I* am lusting after."

Her lips parted, and the desire to slip his tongue into her mouth made him wild. Unfortunately, he couldn't even attempt to kiss her because she turned away from him to open the door. Unlocked. When would Paisley learn to lock her door?

At the threshold, Aster suddenly faced him. "Now I have a question for you."

"Ask."

"What you just said…it confuses me because I wonder, what we have…is it just the relationship between a bodyguard and a principal? And is that all you want? Or…or is it something more? Do you *want* more?"

He shifted closer so that they both stood in the doorway, inches apart. "Do *you* want it to be something more?"

"I do, but I don't have the right to want it because you're not mine."

He wrapped his arms around her, drew her close, and lifted her straight up so that he could peer into her eyes. While he did so, her luscious curves rubbed against him from thighs to chest. The feel of her was exquisite. She wound her arms about his neck, and he held her to him with his arm propping her up under her hips. Gazing into her eyes, he let his impulses take over and slid his fingers through her silky locks. "I am yours, Aster. I am all yours."

Her wings fluttered, riffling her hair. Then she laid a hand to his check, and her thumb skimmed over his skin. The contact had him holding his breath, but Aster's words had him exhaling in a rush. "And I'm yours, Thatch. So completely and utterly yours."

He clenched his jaw while trying to contain his emotions, his needs.

Her voice was so small when she asked, "Can we be official now? You and me?"

Lost for words, he could only nod.

Aster leaned in then and placed her soft lips against his in a kiss that not only stole his breath, but his thoughts and the strength in his legs. He leaned back against the doorframe while accepting that kiss and what it meant. Never did he expect to fall so in love with a fairy. Never did he expect that such a lovely creature could want him in return.

He withdrew his fingers from her hair to hold the back of her head so he could kiss her properly, but not as deeply as he wanted. For Aster, he'd take it slow, however slow she needed. She might be a fairy, but she was a goddess, and he fully intended to treat her as such.

Their lips parted, and he let her slide down his body to her feet. "Have a good night, Aster."

"You, too, Thatch."

When she stepped into the house, he shut the door, eager for the next time he'd see her.

7

Thatch Made of Asters

A week later, they hadn't discussed that kiss or their words on the doorstep. Or done anything more than share that brief moment.

Aster stepped into Thatch's guestroom. He wasn't there. She set a pillow on his bed. The pillow was her excuse to go into his room. She inhaled his scent that still lingered on the air. He smelled like spicy woods—pine and peppercorns and something else, something soft but unidentifiable. She'd tried to figure it out whenever she was around him and had excluded mint, rosemary, lilies, and everything else that had popped into her head. Was it blackberries?

She opened the closet where his clothes hung neatly on hangers and couldn't resist touching the collars of one of his shirts. He always looked so handsome, so put together, so sturdy. She quickly left the closet. Not wanting to get caught, she hurried to the door. Halfway there, though, she halted.

Hanging from the vanity mirror was the daisy chain she'd made him. She skimmed the tip of her finger along the chain, feeling the dried buds. Her heart skipped a beat. *He kept it*. He could've tossed it outside or thrown it in the garbage, but he'd kept it and had draped it over his mirror where he could see it every time he was in this room.

Smiling to herself, she closed the door to his room. On her way to the kitchen, a knock sounded on the front door.

Thatch.

She opened it.

Sure enough, Thatch stood there in navy blue dress pants and a white shirt with the collar unbuttoned and the sleeves rolled to his elbows. Her heart punched her ribcage with passion. *Goddess, he's so handsome.*

"Hi."

He smiled. "Hi there, baby doll."

She stepped closer, testing him.

His body jerked, and she realized he was holding himself back, and had been for the past week. She didn't understand why, so she did what her desires were begging her to do; she embraced his waist and leaned in. "Thatch, will you kiss me?"

His jaw clenched a moment before he molded his hand to the back of her head and bent his neck. She rose up on tiptoe to meet him. Their lips brushed. Then he pressed his lips more firmly to hers while pulling her closer. It was such a simple kiss, no tongue, no heat, even, but she melted into him.

His other hand flattened to the small of her back, and he used that hand to draw her even closer until her breasts pushed against his chest. Still, his hand urged her closer. Her body curled toward him so her pelvis made contact with him. The contact made her gasp. That gasp opened her mouth. With her lips parted, he was able to mold his lips around hers. That intimacy had her clutching him. She'd never been kissed before. Even the kiss they shared in the doorway a week ago hadn't been anything like this. Still, she knew from seeing others kiss that this wasn't even as passionate as it could get. It was enough, though, as she puddled at his feet. He secured his forearm behind her when she struggled to stand upright and sucked on her bottom lip.

Oh my Goddess.

His hand hugging the back of her head began to caress her skull. That tenderness only succeeded in melting her even more. Then his lips shifted to her top lip and formed around it. Her knees buckled. When she lowered a fraction, Thatch's arm contracted and lifted her en pointe, as if she were a ballerina. It took no effort from her to hold that position, because he supported her totally. All she could do was cling to him and experience this kiss with her entire being.

A throat clearing had her jolting, pulling her lips from his, but neither of them stepped away. Her forehead rested against his, and his arm stayed locked behind her, keeping her securely to his body.

"If the two of you could move, I'd be able to go to the meeting."

Paisley's voice penetrated Aster's hazy mind.

She lowered onto the flats of her feet and looked toward Paisley, who wore a red and black tulle dress that was very vampire chic. "Sorry."

Paisley smirked. "Don't be sorry about a kiss like that."

Now it was Thatch clearing his throat. "Would you like me to escort you to the meeting?"

Paisley shook her head. "I'll fly. I'll be there in a few minutes. That is if the two of you don't mind..." She waved her hand, gently indicating that they still needed to move from the doorway.

"Oh, sorry."

Thatch spoke into Aster's ear. "She said not to apologize." Then he picked her up and shifted her out of the way.

"Have a good time," Paisley said while stepping through the doorway. "Don't get into any trouble."

Aster's cheeks burned.

Paisley shut the door behind her.

As soon as they were alone, Thatch's thumb stroked her cheek. "You're gorgeous when you blush."

And her cheeks seared hotter. "I blush a lot."

"I know you do, and I adore it."

Adore? How many demons said 'adore'?

At least one.

Her heart rate increased.

What she had asked him returned to her. *Can we be*

official now? You and me?

At the time, she'd taken his nod to mean everything, but now she needed more. Especially since they'd seemed to go back to bodyguard and principal.

"Thatch, I need to know. Did you mean it? Are we official? Are we together? Because I can't tell."

Thatch stepped right up to her so she had to tilt her head back to peer into his eyes. He met her gaze straight on. "We're together every day, baby doll, exactly how I want it. And, yes, I meant it. I hadn't been able to voice it then, and haven't had the courage since because I've been worried your words were brought on by whatever alcohol you'd had at The Midnight Lair. But that nod, baby doll, was a 'Hell yeah.' I want to be your man, your demon, yours. And I want you to be my woman, my fairy, my everything. Labels are odd for demons, but if you want to label me, call me 'yours.'"

His words came back to her. *I am yours, Aster. I am all yours.*

She had never dreamed of being able to call a demon, or anyone, hers.

Her own words returned to her. *And I'm yours, Thatch. So completely and utterly yours.*

"I meant what I said, too. I want you to call me yours. Please, please, Thatch, call me yours. I want to hear it. I need to hear it."

He snatched her up, back onto tiptoe, and claimed her lips. "Mine." He spoke against her mouth. "Mine, mine, mine."

She became lightheaded while his lips tasted hers and his single, repeated word swirled around and around her like a warm, tingling cocoon. "Yes, yours, mine."

He nodded now and then switched to shaking his head. "Diablo, you have no idea."

"What don't I have any idea about?"

"How much I want you."

She shivered in his embrace.

They were a couple.

Thatch and Aster.

Aster and Thatch.

A smile pulled her lips. She'd been reminded of something that hinted at fate, something she yearned to show him. "I know it's closer to dinner and picnics are usually a lunch thing, but would you like to have a picnic with me?"

His thumb traced her jawline. "Whatever you want."

She fetched a wicker basket. Once the basket was filled with cheese, cold chicken, olives, strawberries, cherries, figs, and chocolate, Thatch hefted it and took her hand. She threaded her fingers with his. They walked through the woods, hand in hand. Thatch wouldn't have agreed to walking in the woods around Paisley's property if it were dangerous. Still, she asked, "Is it safe for us to be out here?"

"I'll protect you with my life, Aster. You're safe with me."

"But I don't want you to get hurt."

He turned to her. "Baby doll, you're mine. I will put my body on the line for you. I will kill anyone who so much as attempts to hurt you. That's a vow I'll live by forever."

She took a shaky breath. "Thatch…"

He set the basket at his feet, cupped her face with his hands, and kissed her until he had her feeling as though she were floating. And still, the kiss wasn't as deep as it could've gone. The thing was, kissing Thatch was like kissing heaven. There didn't need to be tongue involved to have her lightheaded and warm.

After a moment, he pulled back. "Where do you want to have this picnic?"

She pointed. "It's just ahead."

They continued on.

When they reached the spot where she wanted to have the picnic, she indicated at a small bamboo cabin. It had a thatch roof blooming with hundreds of asters. She hadn't been there since she was a kid, hadn't even thought of it until she was giddily repeating *Thatch and Aster, Aster and Thatch* in her head.

"This is where I'd like to eat." She looked at Thatch as he studied the structure. "I hadn't remembered this place until a moment ago, not even when you said your name. It's a thatch." She tilted her head. "I made it when I was little. Well, not the thatch, exactly, but I was practicing my fairy magick and making asters grow through it. I forgot all about it, but it seems that Mother Nature is playing a trick on us."

He finally met her eye. "She's not playing a trick on us. She's blessing us."

Aster bit her bottom lip. "Yes, she is."

He ducked into the cabin, and she followed.

Sitting on the earth floor, they ate their fill and talked about anything and everything.

They were on their first date, and that fact filled

Aster with delight.

He smiled. “Are you happy?”

“Very.”

“Your wings flutter when you’re happy.”

“Yeah.” She glanced over her shoulder. “They always reveal my emotions, little traitors.”

He chuckled. “Don’t call them that. Your wings are beautiful. I like how they mimic what you’re feeling. I’d really love to see what they do when you come.”

She gaped. “W-what?”

He closed his eyes. “I’m sorry. I shouldn’t have said that out loud.”

“How…how often have you thought about that? Me coming?”

His eyelids were still shut. His hands tightened into fists. “Diablo.”

But she needed to know. “How often?”

His eyelids sprang open. “Several times a day.”

“How would you do it?”

He sucked in a breath. “I’ve thought about putting my head under your pretty little dresses and having you come undone on my tongue.”

She blinked. “That could really…make me come?”

He tilted his head. “You’ve never felt…” He looked away and cleared his throat. When he turned back, the look in his eyes stole her breath. “Baby doll, are you a virgin?”

She nodded.

A breath hissed out from between his teeth. “Then you shouldn’t be asking me these questions before you’re ready.”

“Except I am ready.” And she stood. While staring

into his eyes, she reached under the skirt of her dress and pulled her panties down. When they fell around her ankles, she kicked them to the side with a flick of her foot.

His head tilted toward her panties. Then his gaze was on her ankles and slowly rose up her legs to her skirt. Finally, he met her eyes. “Aster.”

She lowered to the floor. Knees bent, she opened her legs. “Show me.”

His chest rose and fell with each breath he took. He scooted closer. His hands closed around her ankles. Staring into her eyes, he widened her legs even more. “I have your permission to look?”

She nodded.

He lifted her skirt over her knees. When his gaze lowered, his mouth fell open. “Your vulva looks like a butterfly.”

She shivered.

His gaze flicked up. “Thank you for showing me. She’s beautiful.”

“Y-you’re welcome.”

“May I kiss it?”

She swallowed. *Holy Goddess*. “Yes, you may.”

He bent down. The warmth of his breath on her leg made her twitch. He planted kisses from the side of her knee to the inside of her right thigh. Then he switched to her left leg, kissing his way up to her inner thigh. Once there, he didn’t stop. The touch of his lips to her clitoris had her gasping. The next kiss was just below her clit. The third right where she throbbed. The fourth lower yet.

When he shifted back, he licked his lips. “You’re

wet, baby doll."

She nodded.

"I don't want to stop kissing it."

"Then don't."

"I want you to come on my tongue."

"So do I."

A growl left him that made her jitter with excitement. That growl was still reverberating through him when he ducked down and planted his head between her thighs. She felt the echoes of his growl right up her center, and it made her whole body vibrate with desire. Then his tongue stroked over her.

She gasped, and her body tensed.

He lifted his head. "Was that okay? Do you want me to stop?"

"No, please don't stop."

"Mm." So, he didn't. He licked her pussy again and again. With each stroke, she relaxed more and more. Never did she think such a thing could feel so amazing, but it did, and it was startling.

She lay back on the earth as she dissolved beneath his tongue. Sighs left her. "Oh, Goddess."

"There you go, baby doll." He spoke with his lips against her and the vibration of his words pried a moan from her. Then his tongue zeroed in on her clitoris. First, the rougher side of his tongue and then the silky underside. Up and down. One after the other.

"Oh, that feels so good."

"Mm." His tongue swirled her clit, and her hips jerked.

When his hands circled around her ankles and lifted her legs onto his shoulders, he feasted more thoroughly.

"Goddess." She couldn't stop her hips from rising off the ground.

He held her hips up while he ate her.

"Goddess."

His lips formed around her clit now and sucked.

Her eyes rolled back. This right here was the epitome of pleasure. She reached out, needing something to grip, and grasped his horns.

"That's it, baby doll."

She moaned.

The sensations she usually felt when she self-pleasured took over her, but far more intense. She ground her hips, pumping them up and down while striving toward the elusive release she'd never experienced before. But as the fluid warmth swirling inside her expanded and the tingling sparks exploded, she doubted she'd really be able to get there.

"Come for me, Aster."

"Oh Goddess. Oh God—" A moan cut off her chant.

His mouth made slurping sounds as he coaxed her to something unknown and magickal and just within reach.

"Don't stop. Don't stop."

He grasped her hips tighter and didn't stop paying her clit all the attention it needed. Pleasure surged up from her core, flooding her entire abdomen and rushed down to her toes as they curled. She had no choice but to release a cry that ripped out of her.

Thatch placed a final kiss to her clit before easing back. "You taste so good, baby doll. And your vulva is so beautiful." He studied it. "I'm going to want her every day. Every single day." He bent down again to place yet another kiss on her vulva. "I'll never get my fill."

"Goddess."

He grinned. "You were so much better than the picnic."

She trembled.

His grin grew. "How are you feeling?"

"Perfect. I've never…what happened at the end there…I've never…" She didn't know how to describe it.

"You orgasmed, baby doll. You've never orgasmed before?"

Sitting up, she smoothed the skirt of her dress over her lap and shook her head. "I've never been able to get myself there." She kept her gaze down as she plucked at the hem of her dress. "It always became too much and I'd stop."

"Well, baby doll, with me, you don't have to do anything but relax and accept, and I'll have you coming anytime you want."

She bit her bottom lip.

He leaned forward and pressed his lips to hers. "I like it when you do that"—he rubbed his thumb over her mouth—"bite this luscious lip of yours."

She lowered her gaze.

He leaned against the bamboo wall. "I like that you're shy with me, but one day, I hope you won't be so shy."

"Stay, and one day I won't be."

"I'm staying, Aster. Even when this threat is gone,

I'll still be here. You're not getting rid of me."

She crawled over to him and cuddled against his side. "I don't want to get rid of you, Thatch."

He put an arm around her.

She laid her head on his shoulder and placed a hand in the middle of his chest. Tucked into his side, she closed her eyes and enjoyed the warmth and solidness of his body and the sense of safety he provided. She was so comfortable, so happy in his embrace that she was drifting off to sleep when he spoke.

"I have something I need to tell you."

"You can tell me anything."

"I know I can, which is why I know I can tell you this." He took a deep breath. "Aster, I'm part fairy."

8

Daggers & Darts

Aster stiffened in his arms, and Thatch squeezed his eyelids shut, hoping his secret wouldn't ruin this. If he lost Aster just as something was forming, he'd never utter those words to another soul again. He'd take his family's secret to his grave.

She pulled away from him, and his arms felt empty.

"What? How?" She shook her head. "What?"

He took another bracing breath. "My grandmother is a fairy."

She blinked. "But I've never heard of any fairy before Paisley's mother having a hybrid child."

"That's because my family was fiercely protective of my grandmother and grandfather. Even the demon side. They didn't want to see either of them hurt or lose the love they had, so they hid the two of them, on the edge of the faye faction. And neither side said a word about them. Not even when they had my father. He looked one-hundred percent demon, so he was raised in the daemon faction, but he was still taught in the way of fairies. Then my father met my mother, a demon, brought her in on the family secret, and they had me. While I am a demon, I take after my faye grandmother in many ways."

The tip of Aster's finger trailed down his forearm, indicating his coloring.

"Yes."

She twirled her finger around the tail of his braid next.

"Yeah."

"And your name?"

"I really was named after my father, Thatcher. My grandparents gave him a name that could pass for a demon name but would hold a bit of faye magick."

She nodded. "You definitely have faye magick in your blood."

He disagreed with a shake of his head. "No magick here, baby doll."

"You're wrong, Thatch. You're full of magick. From the way you play the piano to even how you don't curse or drink."

He grinned. "I never thought of any of that as being from my faye blood."

"They could be. I mean, some fairies curse. I sometimes use naughty words."

He snorted. Although he may not let them slip from his mouth, the thought of her saying naughty words was intriguing.

"And fairies can drink. Mead is a favorite." She waved a hand. "Anyway…" Her words trailed off, and she curled back into his side, settling his worries over losing her because of this secret. "Thank you for telling me." She held on tighter. "I accept you, Thatch. Demon blood, faye blood. I accept every drop that makes you, you. This changes nothing except that I know you a little more."

He kissed the top of her head. "We should get back to Paisley's. The sun is about to set."

She groaned and snuggled closer.

He chuckled. "Do you want me to carry you?"

"Mm. No, I can walk." She got up, fetched her panties, and shook them out.

"Let me."

She paused. "You want to put my underwear on me?"

"You took them off *for me*. I might as well should put them back on you."

"O-okay."

He knelt in front of her. With her hands on his shoulders, he worked her panties around her ankles and slipped them up her legs. Underneath the skirt, with his hands hidden by tulle, he fixed her panties over her lovely butt and followed the band around her hips to make sure they were in the right place. "Is that okay?"

She nodded.

Basket in one hand, his other hand clasping Aster's, they walked back to Paisley's. The sky was a brilliant painting of oranges and pinks when they arrived. As they were stepping up to the door, a moan echoed from somewhere on the property. Thatch froze with horror upon realizing that moan was Paisley's.

"Uh-oh," Aster said. "They're here. Where do you think they are?"

"Knowing the two of them, they could be anywhere."

From the sound of the second moan, they had to be outside. He opened the door and escorted Aster inside. Fast. In the kitchen, they left the picnic basket on the counter, and Thatch snatched up her hand as a distant cry reached them. He hustled her to the guestroom. "We'll be safe in here."

She giggled as she scurried inside.

He shut the door behind them and stood there, watching her as she made her way deeper into his room where he'd been sleeping for days. Every part of his being begged him to pick her up, lay her in the middle of his bed, and cover her with his body. So, he stayed put, watching her.

She paused in front of the mirror. "You kept the daisy chain."

He glanced at the ring of dried flowers. "I did." How could he get rid of anything that Aster had given him, made him? He couldn't.

Aster faced him. "The songs you played on the piano for us at the faye faction, did your grandmother teach you those?"

"She did. Playing those songs for you and the other fairies was the first time I'd played them since I was a boy."

Aster glanced at the daisy chain again. "Are your grandparents still alive?"

"They are. Happily married and living their best lives out of sight. I see them once a month. The next time I go, would you like to meet them?"

Aster's lavender eyes sparkled. "Really?"

"I'd love to introduce them to the fairy I'd die for."

"Thatch." Her voice was a whisper.

He took a step. "I'd love to introduce them to the fairy who makes me happier than I have ever been my entire life."

She hadn't moved. "Thatch."

Another step. "I'd love to introduce them to the fairy I can see myself with for the rest of my life."

"Thatch."

He cradled her face with his hands. "But only if you'd want to meet them."

She nodded. "I would. I really would."

Thatch leaned in.

Aster's hands on his chest halted him. "What was that?"

"What was what?"

"Sounded like someone yelled my name."

They both stilled.

Then it came. "Aster!"

"It's Case." Thatch flung the door open.

Aster ran out ahead of him.

"Aster!"

They raced in the direction of Case's shouts.

Aster shoved open the kitchen door and froze. "Oh my—" She covered her mouth with her hand.

Paisley was sitting on the countertop with Case's suit jacket draped over her shoulders. Her legs, from the tips of her toes to mid-thighs, were scorched with burns. Blackened flesh. Raw skin oozing blood.

Thatch took in the scene while every fiber of his being activated with the need to protect. Flames snaked along the tile, feeding off a brown liquid. Broken glass flashed among the fire. The window was smashed.

Molotov cocktail.

"Stay with them," Case ordered and leapt through that broken window.

Thatch wanted nothing more than to join him and make whoever had done this pay, but he couldn't leave them. Wouldn't.

Aster dashed forward while tugging the satchel loose from her waist. She shoved her hand inside and quickly tossed fairy dust onto Paisley's legs.

On the countertop, Paisley shook like a leaf.

He went over to her and put a hand on her back. "It's okay."

He rubbed her back, hoping to calm her. Seeing Paisley hurt snapped something in him, just as he knew it had snapped something in Case. Paisley was so strong. She was a queen, for Diablo's sake, and there she was, sitting on her own kitchen counter, injured from what was clearly an assassination attempt, with tears in her eyes from the pain and trauma of it. And there was Aster, healing her best friend and holding herself together while doing it, even though her wings were shivering from the emotions she was keeping contained within her petite body.

"We'll figure out who did this. I swear to you both that this won't go unanswered."

The burns were disappearing as more fairy dust fell from Aster's fingers.

But Paisley was still shaking.

Tears still filled her eyes.

Aster's wings still quivered.

He moved his hand in a soothing circular motion on Paisley's back and reached out to squeeze Aster's shoulder.

Hand trembling, she pulled more fairy dust from her satchel.

Case climbed back through the window.

"Anything?" Thatch asked.

Case answered with a shake of his head.

Damn it.

Aster looked to Thatch. The fear in her eyes gutted him.

"Why don't the two of you go into the parlor so we can clean this up and patch up the window?"

She nodded. "Okay, yeah." And held out a hand to Paisley.

Paisley didn't say a word when she accepted Aster's hand.

Thatch watched them leave and hated how Paisley emitted defeat. He didn't know what to say about that defeat or the fear that swallowed Aster or the rage and defeat and fear seeping off Case. So, he stayed silent while they cleaned up the glass and liquor and secured the window with a piece of plywood from the shed.

In the parlor, the women they cared about were

huddled on the love seat, looking so fragile that he wanted to murder the bastard who caused that. He lowered stiffly onto the chair across from Aster. What proceeded was a discussion about Paisley choosing to stay in her home, which he couldn't fault her for, and Case informing them that the Molotov cocktail had been made of dragon's breath. He'd felt it against his wings, and Thatch believed him.

When Paisley left to go upstairs, Aster revealed that Paisley had been there when her father had been incinerated in a similar fashion—with a dragon's breath Molotov cocktail.

That secret was too heavy for them all. Most of all Case, who left to check on Paisley.

Thatch got up to take the seat beside Aster, and she burrowed into his side.

"That was terrifying."

He swooped his arms around her and pulled her onto his lap. "I know, baby doll, I know. We're going to do everything we can to protect Paisley. And you."

She nodded with her head buried in the side of his neck.

"With the kitchen compromised, and after what happened, I'm going to sleep in here, guard the windows and doors."

"I'll sleep in here, too."

"No, you'll be safer in your room."

"I'll be safer with you. Anyone could break in through my balcony."

He clenched his jaw at the truth of her words.

"But if someone broke in here, you'd be here with me."

He tightened his arms around her. "And no one will be able to get past me to touch you. I can promise you that."

"I know. I trust you, Thatch. With my life, with all of me, I trust you."

He squeezed his eyelids shut. Her words meant the world to him. "Alright, baby doll." He caressed her back. "Let's get some blankets and pillows." No matter how much he would like Aster to sleep on his lap, on his chest, for him to stay vigilant, it'd be better if there was a little distance between them. He couldn't protect her from an assassin if she lay on top of him. Well, he could…by switching their positions and putting his back to the assassin, but a sword through his back could reach Aster. It'd be best if she had a chance to run, so they got blankets and pillows. "You can fit on the couch. I'll sleep on the floor."

"Okay." She lay on her side, curled up beneath a blanket, and he stretched out on his back, with the small blanket pulled to the middle of his chest. "Thatch?"

"Hm?"

"I need to touch you."

Diablo. He needed to touch her, too, so he reached up, took her hand off the couch cushion, and brought it to his lips to kiss her fingers. Then he held her hand. "Is this okay?"

"This is perfect. Night, Thatch."

"Goodnight, baby doll."

In the morning, Thatch made a quick trip to Case's to get reports from the council. Someone had to have something by now. With how many demons they had out there, there was no way a threat like this could stay hidden for long.

Except, none of them had any clue as to who'd tried to kill Paisley last night. That wouldn't sit well with Case. Hell, it didn't sit well with Thatch.

A banging on the front door drew him from the conference room. He stepped out into the hall in time to hear Case tell Jude, Centaur King and Paisley's godfather, that he was going to the fier faction because dragon fire could mean Queen Enya was behind the attack. Except, Paisley had no idea Case intended to avenge her, and he had a feeling Paisley wouldn't be pleased that Case was doing something so extreme without her.

Knowing that, Thatch couldn't stay silent. "As your right-hand, it's my job to tell you when you're making a big mistake…and you're making a big mistake."

Case turned. His posture was stiff, clearly not liking that his right-hand and best friend was pointing out that his plan was the wrong one to make.

But Thatch couldn't let this go unsaid. "Not telling Paisley, going behind her back…not smart."

"I'm doing what I have to do."

Thatch lifted a hand. He could understand that need for revenge, but he couldn't understand the secrecy. And Paisley certainly wouldn't forgive that. "Whatever, it's your decision, it's your funeral." Because although he didn't know Paisley well, he knew her enough that he was positive she wouldn't forgive Case for doing this behind her back. Not after she'd almost been killed.

Case and Jude were going, though. No matter what he said.

"I know Aster is your priority, but can you keep an eye on Paisley for me while I'm gone?" That request from Case spoke volumes. Case wouldn't trust Paisley's safety with just anyone, and Thatch would take that mission as seriously as the one to protect Aster. Except, Paisley wasn't Aster. She was a free spirit. She didn't want a bodyguard.

Thatch bowed his head. "If she lets me, I will."

"Thank you."

And off Case and Jude went.

Thatch exhaled. This wasn't going to end well. He returned to Paisley's to find the two of them in the kitchen. Aster was cutting up fruit and adding the sweet morsels to a large bowl. A pile of banana peels, strawberry leaves, kiwi skins, and cherry stems sat next to a wood cutting board. Next to her, Paisley was scrambling eggs in a frying pan on the stovetop.

Aster gave him the sweetest smile. "Good morning."

"Morning."

Paisley looked over her shoulder. "Hey, Thatch." She shifted back to the eggs. "Did you see Case? Before he left, he said he'd be sending demons to stand guard around the property."

"That's right. They're in position now. I saw them when I returned."

"He also said that you'd be here inside with us."

"That's right," he repeated and glanced at Aster.

"I'm not going anywhere."

"Did Case tell you when he'd be back?"

"No."

Paisley turned with a wooden spoon in her hand. The tip had dried egg stuck to it. "If the demons are already in place, what else does he have to do?"

Thatch lifted a shoulder.

Paisley lowered the wooden spoon. In her eyes, he could tell she was piecing together what he wasn't saying. "He's doing something about the attempt last night, isn't he? And he doesn't want me to know."

Aster laid down the knife she'd been using to slice a banana and faced him.

"Isn't he?" Paisley asked.

Case may be his lord, but he couldn't lie. Not to them. "He is."

"What is he doing?"

Thatch didn't answer.

Paisley reached out and turned off the burner with a loud snap. "What is he doing, Thatch?"

Thatch exhaled. "He's going to the fier faction."

"Goddess," Aster whispered.

He glanced at her and back to Paisley. "Case wants to question them." He took a small step. "He's strong in his belief that it was dragon's breath, and he will do anything to find out if the dragons were behind the attempt. If someone had tried to kill Aster last night with a dragon's breath Molotov cocktail, I'd be doing the same thing."

"But would you have kept it a secret from her?" Paisley demanded.

He met Aster's eye now. "No. I couldn't keep that

from her."

"What does it mean that Case could…and did?"

"I don't know. I don't pretend to know what goes on in Case's head. I might've known him since we were twelve, but"—he shook his head—"Case does what he wants to. I don't have the power to sway him."

Paisley stared at the eggs in the frying pan. After a moment, she set the wooden spoon on the counter. "Excuse me." She walked past him.

Aster stepped up to him. "This isn't good. She values honesty above most everything else. She's been betrayed before." Aster's violet hair streamed off her shoulder when she shook her head. "This isn't good."

Over the next few hours, he realized how right she was. Paisley spent that time outside, attacking a target with her daggers over and over again. She was so relentless about it that she'd severed the target in half and replaced it with a fresh one.

Thatch kept an eye on her from a balcony, and he could see the demons posted nearby looking at him with a twinge of fear in their eyes. Would Paisley throw the next dagger at them? No one knew. She kept at it long past when someone's arms would've grown tired. Each strike was perfectly aimed—smack-dab in the center. A second target sliced down the middle, and she retrieved another from the gardening shed.

"She could do this all day."

Thatch peered over his shoulder at Aster.

"This is what she does. When she finds it hard to cope with something."

Thatch sighed. "You said this isn't good. How bad is this exactly?"

"On a scale from one to ten? Eleven."

He gripped the rail. Case could be gone for days. Thatch had to figure out some way to calm things down until he returned. "I'll try to talk to her."

"She's lethal *without* daggers, Thatch."

"I'll be okay." He made his way down to where Paisley was actively attempting to demolish a third target. "Paisley?"

She stiffened. "Thatch, this is me trying to vent."

"I know. It's just...you've been out here a long time. It's not safe. Come inside. Get some water."

"I'm fine."

"No, you're not."

She spun toward him. "And you know why I'm not, don't you?"

"I don't know what you and Case have together."

"Then let me tell you. We had an agreement. We never promised to be truthful to each other, but we made other promises. Not a single one of those matter, because how could they when the other person a part of that will just go off and leave you without a fucking word? Well, now I'm going to have the last word. The next time you see him, tell him the arrangement is over." She tugged the daggers from the target, jammed them into the holsters at her thighs, and stormed past him.

"Shit." He dug out his cell phone from his pocket and called Case, who answered immediately.

"Hey, is everything okay?" The worry in Case's voice said more than his words did, even more than his actions. Case cared about Paisley and feared for her life. That was far more evident now than ever before.

Case cared about her, and now Thatch had to tell him that Paisley didn't want anything to do with him anymore.

He ran a hand over his face. "I'm not sure if I would describe this as okay."

"What do you mean? Did something happen?"

Thatch let out a breath. "You could say that. Paisley asked me where you were, so I told her the truth. I wasn't going to lie. She's pissed, Case, as I knew she would be. She told me that the next time I talk to you to say these words exactly, 'The arrangement is over.'"

"Are you there now?"

"I am."

"Give her your phone. I'll talk to her."

"Alright."

Thatch walked back into the house and found Paisley sipping water in the parlor. Without a word, he held the phone out to her.

"Who is it?" She took the phone from him and looked at the screen where Case's name was displayed. "You've got to be kidding me." She jabbed her finger onto the screen and tossed the phone at him.

He caught it against his chest.

"Don't try to trick me, Thatch. Don't do that." And she shouldered past him.

Eyes closed, he stood there, hating himself. And, frankly, despising Case.

His phone rang. He answered it without even bothering to look at who the caller was. "I knew that'd go that way."

"Find her and put me on speaker."

Thatch shook his head. "I told you this would be your funeral. Don't make it mine, too."

A gentle hand touched his arm.

He opened his eyes to see Aster in front of him. "Give it to me."

He passed her the phone.

She pressed it to her ear. "What do you need me to do?"

Thatch followed Aster into the kitchen where she held up the phone. "Go."

"Paisley—"

The sound of Case's voice had Paisley shoving off the stool she occupied. "Oh my Goddess. You and Thatch need to stop. I don't want to talk to him. He made his choice. He left."

"I didn't leave *you*."

Case's claim had her stilling.

"I left, yes, but I left to find out where the dragon's breath came from."

She stomped up to the phone Aster held out and spoke into the speaker. "You did it behind my back, Case. My parents kept me in the dark, too, because they thought it was for my own good. And, in the end, that's what got them killed. I already asked you not to leave me out of anything that has to do with threats against me. I *asked* you. Going behind my back, like you did, is something I will never tolerate. In case Thatch didn't already tell you, I'll say it now, and it's the last thing I'm going to say to you…our arrangement is over." Then she snatched the phone from Aster, ended the call, and slammed it onto the table. Her burgundy eyes met them next. “Don’t. Do. That. Again.” She stormed out of the kitchen.

A moment later, a door upstairs slammed.

9

12 Pink Roses, 9 Red, 1 White

Case had been gone for two days, but the damage had been done. When he returned, Paisley refused to see him. For three long weeks. Thatch stayed at Paisley's every moment, and it wasn't just for Aster anymore, which she understood. He had to protect Paisley, too. Without Case there, someone had to do it, but Paisley didn't exactly make it easy. She stood outside, just as easy a target as the targets she impaled with her daggers.

When she wasn't doing that, she was holed up in her room.

Aster tried to get Paisley to come out, to spend time with her and Thatch, but Paisley declined. Aster had never seen Paisley like this. No man, regardless of what faction he was from, had ever impacted Paisley so much. It got so bad that Paisley's health was affected. Her skin paled. Her eyes dimmed. She needed to feed on blood, but she refused to do that, too.

Before Case, Paisley had struggled to feed because, as part-fairy, it went against her nature. Then she'd started to feed off Case, and that had eased her dilemma, but now…Paisley's stomach couldn't tolerate any blood that wasn't Case's. No matter what Aster did, no matter what blood she acquired, it didn't help. Not even AB Negative blood from a teenage human did the trick. Aster was terrified for Paisley. So terrified that she did something behind Paisley's back.

She removed her phone from her pouch and called the one person who could fix this. "Case? You told me to call you if there's a sign of danger."

"What's going on?"

"It's Paisley. You saw her today at the Enchanted Hierarchy Council Meeting. She's not well, Case. She won't admit it, but she needs you. She needs to feed. I'm afraid that if she doesn't get blood today she's going to…" She couldn't voice the consequences. Paisley could fall into a coma, and not even a blood transfusion would help her then.

"I'm coming."

Those two words relieved Aster more than any other two words ever had.

A moment later, Case arrived. "Where is she?"

"Out back. She wants to tend to her roses." Aster wrung her hands. "She's so weak that being in the sun…" A shake of her head, and she hoped she conveyed the seriousness of the matter.

"I'll take care of her." And Case headed out back.

Aster went to Thatch and burrowed into him. "I'm so glad he came."

His wide hand stroked her back. "Me, too. But you know…if she doesn't kill him, they're going to…"

She knew exactly what he was hinting at. "The only safe place is my room. We could hole up in there."

"We might want to hurry."

Laughing, she led him into her room and shut the door behind them. Seeing him there, beside her bed, sent flutters throughout her body. She hoped her wings weren't betraying what she felt on the inside, but then she felt the gentle breeze against the backs of her shoulders and knew they were fluttering, too.

"Do you have music to drown them out?"

She opened an app on her phone and scrolled through her playlists.

As she searched for one, Thatch's hands swallowed her shoulders. His breath warmed the shell of her ear. "Why are your wings fluttering like this?"

The edges of her wings skimmed over Thatch's shirt and chest. She quickly selected a playlist with plenty of piano solos and turned up the volume.

Thatch rotated her around. "They're still fluttering."

She nodded. "Because of you."

He brushed her hair behind her, leaned down, and kissed the curve of her shoulder. Kiss by kiss, he made his way up the side of her neck. Then he cradled her jaw with his hand and drew her in for a kiss that had her wings fluttering faster.

"You're floating," he said against her lips.

She glanced down. Sure enough, she was hovering a few inches off the floor. "A kiss like that would have anyone walking on air." She forced her wings to calm until her feet settled on the floor. Then she drew him over to her bed, crawled onto the mattress, and patted the place next to her. "Lie down with me."

He took the spot beside her.

She cuddled against him with her head on his chest.

They lay there, listening to the music, but not even the piano could calm Aster, because all she could think about was that Thatch was in her bed. Then there was Paisley's cry outside. The sound of her best friend in the throes of passion with Case brought back the memory of what she'd felt when Thatch went down on her and how loud her own cries had been. That memory brought the one of Thatch on her balcony, stroking himself while thinking of her. She wanted to know if she could get him to make the same noises as Case was making now.

"Diablo." Thatch took her phone and increased the volume.

She giggled. But not even laughter could erase her urges. She moved her hand in circular patterns over his ribs and abs. Goddess, the feel of the muscles his shirt hid. She continued to rub those hard muscles, working her way to his pants. With her head on his chest, she was able to watch her hand as she touched, caressed. She slipped her hand down his right thigh and then back up. Again, she glided her hand down his thigh, but this time when she drew her hand up, she curled her hand over the inside of his thigh and slid her palm along the length of his cock nestled against that thick thigh. Back and forth, she massaged his hardening cock through his pants.

Thatch groaned. “Aster.”

She dragged down the zipper of his pants and dipped her hand through the opening. Against her fingertips, his cock felt hot. She curled her fingers around him and couldn’t quite get her fingertips to touch. In her fist, he was so hard, so thick. She’d never felt anything like it. When she stroked him, he let loose a growl that gave Aster a rush of power. Never had she been the reason for such a sound.

A hiss escaped him. “Aster.”

She sat up to peer down at him as she stroked his length. His pupils were dilated. His cheeks were flushed a darker purple. Goddess, he was so handsome. She worked open the belt and button of his pants and parted the sides so that his cock was free to stand tall, and stand tall it did. Beneath that plush blanket, she’d been amazed at the size of his erection. Now, in front of her, the length of his penis was amazing and a little startling. She curled her fingers around him and witnessed her hand as she slowly pumped it up and down. Her pale fingers against the violet skin of his cock was beautiful.

He was staring at her hand, too. "Aster. Diablo, that feels so good. Don't stop." Now he was the one begging her, just as she had begged him not to stop when his mouth was on her pussy.

"I'm not going to stop, Thatch. I want you to come in my hand, like you came in yours. On my balcony."

His gaze met hers. "So, you did see me?"

She bit her bottom lip and nodded. "I couldn't look away then." She shifted her gaze back to his beautiful penis. "I can't look away now." And she stroked his cock faster. "I like how you feel in my hand." But what would he feel like inside her? Her curiosity was strong enough to have her going wet with desire.

Thatch began to lift his hips, thrusting his cock in her fist. Seeing his hips jutting with the need to orgasm in her hand was the sexiest thing she'd ever seen. His grunts filled her ears. They were a purely erotic melody that she wanted to keep on hearing, like a never-ending orchestra.

"Aster…Aster…"

She never knew the sensual magic of hearing someone use her name as a chant while feeling pleasure, and she was glad it was Thatch.

"Aster…Aster…"

His hips stuttered, and his cock jerked. A creamy, white substance shot from the tip of his penis. He let out a moan that echoed in her bedroom as that warm creaminess streamed over her fingers. When his orgasm ended, he tucked his penis into his pants and got up.

In her adjoining bathroom, he wet a small towel and brought it back. He cleaned his cum off her fingers himself. Then he stretched out on top of her and kissed her good and long. So good and long that she melted beneath him.

He pushed up onto his forearms. “You’re gorgeous.”

She smiled. “So are you.”

He laughed. “I’ve never been called gorgeous before.”

“I will call you that every day if you’d like.” She pulled his braid from off his shoulder and played with the silky end. “Because you are.”

“Thank you, but you’re far more gorgeous.”

“Debatable.” She twirled the end of his braid around her finger. “Did I…did I do that right…when I…?”

“Yeah, baby doll, you did that right.”

Her cheeks burned.

Thatch leaned down and pressed his lips to her cheeks one at a time.

A door opened and closed somewhere beyond Aster’s room.

“I think they’re done. Or at least they’ve moved indoors.” He kissed the middle of her forehead. “I’m going to run a quick errand.”

Now? What could he need to do right this second?

Disappointment flooded her. “Oh, okay.” She had wanted to stay in bed with him, but now he was leaving.

He kissed her hand, the one that had been wrapped around his cock. “I’ll be right back.”

“Okay.”

She watched him leave. If she’d gotten up the courage to tell him how much she wanted him in that moment, would he have stayed?

Sighing, she dragged herself out of bed and into the bathroom where she washed her hands and any evidence that Thatch had aroused her while she got him off. Then she stood in her room, wondering what to do now that she was alone.

Cooking and baking were the two things she liked to do to get her mind off whatever was bothering her, so she retreated to the kitchen. A peek through the door showed it was empty, and she hunkered down with flour, sugar, and butter. She took out a muffin tin. In a bowl, she sifted together the dry ingredients, added milk until the mixture was a perfect wetness, and then folded in fresh blueberries and cranberries. She was scooping the mixture into muffin tins when the front door opened and closed.

"Aster?" Thatch's voice carried over to her.

She paused. Thatch leaving had bothered her, but he hadn't been gone long, as he'd promised. She took a deep breath before answering. "Kitchen."

The door swung open, and Thatch stood there with an arm behind his back. "What are you doing?"

"Baking muffins for tomorrow morning. Do you like muffins?"

"I do." His arm looped around her, and he held a white rose in front of her.

She froze.

"One white rose for love at first sight, pure and innocent. When I saw you the first time, baby doll, I knew right away that I not only wanted you but *needed* you."

She took the white rose with a trembling hand.

"It's beautiful."

Thatch kissed her shoulder. "I'm not done."

A bouquet of pink roses appeared before her.

"Twelve pink roses for the happiness I feel and because I can call you mine."

Her heart beat fast against her chest. She hugged the roses to herself and buried her nose in the soft petals. "Mm." She inhaled long and deep. Then she turned. "You left to get me roses?"

"I'd never leave you for anything less."

"But to leave while we were in bed together?"

"I had to leave."

She frowned. "What? Why?"

"Because I wanted to make love to you."

She gaped. "Then why…why didn't you?"

He curled his left hand around her waist. "Because I don't want to hurt you."

Her frown returned. "Why would you hurt me?"

"I wouldn't do it on purpose, but…you saw my erection, baby doll." His hand contracted on her waist. "You're so petite. I *would* hurt you."

She stared at the dozen pink roses and single white rose in her hands. "You don't know that."

"But I do. You're tiny, and I'm big. You're a virgin, and…I'd hurt you." He shook his head. "I can't hurt you."

The rejection was a quick pang in the middle of her chest.

A tear slipped down her cheek as she kept her gaze on the roses, hoping Thatch wouldn't see it, but he did.

His fingers cradled her chin, and he raised her face. "What is this?" He swiped the tear from her skin. "Why are you crying?"

Her lips trembled. "Are you breaking up with me?"

He moved his right arm out from behind his back. A rustling sound met her ears as he set something on the counter beside her. Then he was embracing her to his body. "Why would you think that?"

"If we can't be together…fully be together…why would you want to stay?"

"I'm not a sex demon, baby doll. I don't require sex in a relationship. I don't need it to survive. What we have is enough for me. Could it be enough for you?"

"I think so. I just…I want you to be happy."

"I *am* happy. I am so completely happy. That's what the pink roses were for. And…" He reached to the counter and picked up another bouquet. "Nine red roses for eternal love."

Her breath left her. "You got me all of these roses to—"

"Tell you how much you mean to me."

More tears filled her eyes. "They're beautiful. You're beautiful. I…should I get you flowers in return?"

He smiled. "No, all I need is—" He lifted her onto her toes and kissed her. "That's all I need, baby doll. That's all I need."

She was clutching the roses between them. "After the muffins are done, would you like to stay the night with me? In my bed?"

He sucked in a breath. "Yeah, I would.

10

Marshmallow Demon

Aster wore a peach-toned silk nightgown that clung to her breasts, slid over her shapely hips, and circled around her ankles. Her violet hair was piled atop her head, showing off the length of her neck, her collarbones, and the curves of her shoulders. She was stunning, and she stole Thatch's breath.

"How do you want to do this, baby doll?"

Wings tucked against her back, she crawled beneath the blanket. As she did so, the bodice of her dress plunged, and he was awarded with the sight of her full breasts and that peach-toned silk fighting to cover her nipples.

His dick thickened inside his sweatpants.

She lay flat on her back and opened her arms. “Come here. Like how we were earlier.”

He climbed onto the bed and positioned himself over her. Holding himself up with one hand, he brought the other to her breast. The shape and weight of her breast, with the hard nub of her nipple digging into the center of his palm, had a growl of hunger rumbling in his chest. He hooked the thin strap of her nightgown and drew it down her arm until the silk pulled back from her breast. His mouth watered at the sight of it. So round. So beautiful. He traced her areola with the tip of his finger. “What color would you call this?”

She peered at her breast as he continued to draw circles around her nipple. “Um. I don’t know. Taupe.”

He captured her nipple between his thumb and index finger. “And this color?”

“Mauve taupe, maybe.”

“I like this color. I want—” He licked his lips. “I want your breast in my mouth. No…*need*.” And he bent down to fuse his lips around her breast. So soft. So yielding. He sucked on her breast, pulling her nipple into his mouth.

She moaned and arched her back.

He braced his arms behind her to hold her against him as he feasted. But the more he sucked on her breast, the more ravenous he became. He moaned with her. Greedy and hard, he rubbed his tongue over her nipple, coaxing more sighs from her. The little noises she made were like a siren’s song.

More, please more. He sought her other breast with his hand. Watching the peach-toned silk slide away from her curves and the peak of her nipple made him impossibly hard. “Diablo. You have amazing breasts, baby doll.” And he formed his mouth around her other breast now to savor, to lavish, to adore.

While he tasted her nipple, he glided his hand up her thigh.

Her legs parted.

The silk nightgown bunched around his wrist as he moved his hand higher. When his fingertips grazed the inside of her thigh, her leg shook. He caressed her vulva. “Diablo, you’re wet.” He gazed into her eyes while he followed the butterfly lips of her labia. “You feel so good.”

“So do your fingers.” She fisted her hands into the bedding beneath her. “Oh, Goddess.”

He swirled the tip of his finger around her opening. “I want to feel inside you, baby doll. Do I have your permission?” He probed her entrance. When she jerked her hips off the bed, his fingertip sank in to the top of his nail.

Aster trembled. “More, please more.”

It was exactly what he’d thought a moment ago. Maintaining eye contact, he gently slid his finger deeper. She was so tight around his finger, and that tightness only increased as her flesh stretched for his first knuckle. Her mouth opened, and a soft gasp expelled from her lips.

He paused. “Are you okay, baby doll?”

She nodded. “Don’t stop.”

He continued to slip his finger into her until he was in her to his last knuckle. “You feel that?” He eased his finger out and then back in. “How tight you are?”

She nodded again while biting her bottom lip.

"That's just my finger, baby doll. Just my finger. Does it hurt?"

"Um…n-not much. A little."

"That's why I'm worried, but I *can* do this." And he guided his finger in and out of her again. "And I can do this." He swirled his fingertip over her internal flesh. "Tell me when you feel something. Something good." He shifted his finger slightly this way and that, searching for the spot that would have her shaking with pleasure. He knew instantly when he found it because her hips rolled and she inhaled sharply.

"There. Right there. That feels…that feels…"

"Mm." He nibbled on her jawline. "Come for me, baby doll. I want you to come on my finger. I want to feel your muscles squeezing my knuckle."

"Yes, daddy."

Thatch stilled.

"Did you just call me *daddy*?"

The smile she gave him made him even harder.

"Diablo." He tugged the blanket from her body, shoved up her nightgown, and ducked his head to suck on her pretty little clit. The second he ran his tongue over the bud, she cried out. He alternated between sucking on and licking her clit with his tongue while his finger relentlessly massaged her g-zone. Her moans in his ear had pre-cum gushing from his penis and a roar of pleasure erupting from him. She stunned him by coming right then.

He would've loved to eat her out for so much longer, but her vagina was clenching his finger, and she was crying out her release. He sat up. "You feel so good squeezing my finger."

She let out another tiny moan.

"I'm going to pull my finger out now."

She nodded.

He withdrew his finger slowly.

A breath escaped her.

"Are you still okay?"

She nodded again.

"You came fast, baby doll. I was hoping to do that for a little longer."

She fixed her nightgown. "Your fault."

He arched a brow. "My fault?"

"Mm-hm. You growled against my pussy. I felt it vibrate deep inside and—" She mimed an explosion. "Apparently your moans are all I need."

"It was your cries that made me pre-cum, so I'd say it's your fault."

"Then I accept my part in it."

Grinning, he tapped his lips to hers. "Speaking of, I have to clean up."

In the bathroom, he washed away his pre-cum and lathered his hands. He was still hard when he returned to the bed, and Aster's gaze was on it.

"Thatch, you're still—"

"I know." He stretched out on the bed and tucked her close to his body. "It'll go down. I just want to hold you. May I hold you?"

"All night, Thatch." She snuggled against his chest. "Hold me all night long."

His erection did eventually go down, and he drifted off to sleep. He slept better that night than any night before. All because a gorgeous fairy slept in his arms. Come morning, he was lightheaded with love. And that gorgeous fairy was still beside him. He kissed her shoulder.

She hummed.

"I'm going to shower. Stay warm in bed."

She hummed again.

Smiling to himself, he left her bedroom, went to the guest bath, showered, and changed. Instead of finding Aster still snuggled beneath her blanket, she was awake and pulling on one of her tiny dresses.

"I told you to stay warm in bed."

She peered over her shoulder. "I'm an early riser. I love mornings." She reached behind her for the zipper of her dress.

"I got that." He held the two sides of her dress together and drew the zipper up to her wings. "I will be your personal dress zipper-upper every morning. And every evening, I'll be your personal dress zipper-downer."

She faced him. "My zippers are going to be your responsibility now?"

"That's right, baby doll."

She glided her palm up and down his chest. "I never knew a bodyguard's duties were so extensive."

"Well, I take my bodyguard duties seriously."

"And I'm grateful for that. Breakfast?"

"I *am* hungry."

"I'm talking about food."

"Lead the way."

She led him to the kitchen. The entire way, he couldn't stop from eyeing the hem of her dress and the lovely shape of her hips.

"Thatch, are you ogling me?"

"Oh yeah."

She laughed.

They sat at the kitchen table eating the blueberry and cranberry muffins Aster had made yesterday. Not long later, Paisley and Case joined them. Paisley didn't stay long, though. When Case didn't trot after her immediately, Thatch was surprised. He was surprised again when Case did eventually leave and came back a moment later demanding for Aster to give Paisley a blood transfusion. His face was pale, and fear reflected in his eyes. Thatch had never seen Case as terrified. What in the world could cause that level of terror?

Aster dashed out of the kitchen, causing the spikes to clatter together in the bag tied at her waist, and Thatch shoved to his feet to follow.

Case's hand lifting to bar him from following Aster halted him. He didn't only stop because Case was his boss giving an order, but because if he got any closer, he'd be breaking his boss's hand for daring to block him from Aster.

"No," Case said with a hand up to stop him. "Stay here."

Thatch fought to keep his hands from forming into fists. "Case, with all due respect, I looked out for both of them while you were gone, and the month she refused to see you. She's as much my responsibility as Aster is." And he wouldn't do anything to harm that; he wasn't as reckless as Case.

"I appreciate that you looked out for her when I couldn't, but I don't think she'd want you there now."

Thatch tilted his head. "But she needs a blood transfusion?"

"She does."

Needing blood was abnormal, and Paisley needing blood when she looked fine a moment ago was alarming. "Was she injured?"

"No. It's her moon time, and…"

Thatch nodded. He knew how much fairies revered their moon times, and he was aware that such a thing could be different for Paisley, given her vampire half. Fatal, even. And if Paisley were hurt, Aster would be worried sick. "I want to be close to Aster."

Case returned the nod. "Alright. You can post outside the room."

Not arguing with that, he took the place outside the door, returning to his guard duties. From his place, he listened to the conversation on the other side. Paisley was trying to convince Case that she was okay, and Case wasn't hearing it. He told Aster to hook him up, and Thatch could only imagine that meant Case would be on the other end of the transfusion.

Several minutes later, Aster tiptoed out of the room and went right to Thatch. He held her close. "Is she okay?"

Beneath his hand, Aster shook her head. "I don't know. I'm giving Case fifteen minutes." She removed her phone from her pouch and set the timer. "I hope that's going to be enough."

"It will. Let's give them some privacy."

Downstairs, Aster's wings were pointed high, stiff, and quivering. She was terrified, and Thatch hated that. He curled his hands around her shoulders and glided them slowly down her arms. "I know you're scared, but Case has her, and I have you. Neither one of us is going to let anything happen to either of you."

"This is different, Thatch. Her aversion to blood and her moon time…they're not assassins you can fight. They're not bad guys you can threaten. They're shitty cards she was given by the Goddess, and sometimes I don't get why—" Her voice choked up.

"Ssh." He turned her to face him. "The Goddess has her own reasons." He glanced up the stairs. "And maybe that reason was Case."

A tiny smile lifted Aster's pretty pink lips. "Yeah…maybe." Her smile widened. "I like that. The two of them are perfectly imperfect together. They work. Even if they don't want to admit it."

"They will one day."

"You're a true romantic, Thatch."

He combed his fingers through her hair. "You're just now realizing that?"

"No, I'm just now pointing it out." She peered upstairs again. "He really cares about her. She'll have a hard time with that, but I don't think her stubbornness will force him to back down at all. She needs that. She needs someone who won't back down."

"Case definitely is not one to back down from a challenge." Thatch cupped her head with his hand. "So, you were telling me what Paisley needs. What do *you* need?"

"I need *you*, Thatch. Everything I've ever dreamed about when it comes to a relationship…you embody it all. You're all I need."

He lifted her off the floor and held her against his chest. "You've got me."

Her wings twittered in a flirtatious way. She slung

her arms around his neck. “And you’ve got me. Figuratively *and* literally.”

His arms flexed. “I like holding you. I could hold you all day.” He touched his lips to hers and spoke against her mouth. “And all night.”

“I like the sound of that.”

He drew her into a long, lingering kiss.

She sighed. “Are you trying to distract me from what’s happening?”

“Is it working?”

“A little.” She checked the timer on her phone. “But if you really want me distracted for the next thirteen minutes, I have another idea.”

“What is it? I’ll do anything.”

“It’s not what you need to do, but what you need to *let* me do.”

He cocked a brow. “This is sounding dirty.”

Her laughter was lyrical. “It’s not. I…I’d like to braid your hair. I’ve been wanting to touch your hair since…well, since we met.”

His brows lowered. “Why didn’t you tell me sooner?”

“Telling someone you just met that you want to touch their hair, people will look at you like a weirdo.”

“A beautiful fairy like you? You tell someone you want to touch their hair, and that person will lay their head in your lap and let you touch their hair until they fall asleep and your fingers are tired.”

She smiled. “There’s only one person whose hair I want to touch.”

He carried her into the kitchen, set her on her feet, and lowered onto a stool. “Then touch away, baby doll."

"Really?"

"Do whatever you want with my hair."

"Okay." She removed the tie at the end of his braid and combed her fingers through his hair. "Your hair is so beautiful."

"*Your* hair is beautiful."

She continued to slide her fingers through his hair. "When I try to compliment you, you turn it around to me. Why can't you take a compliment?"

He shrugged. Compliments made him feel awkward, but how to explain that to a fairy who likely received compliments everywhere she went, and deservedly so. But that was the difference between fairies and demons. Fairies were naturally sweet and giving creatures. Demons were naturally abrasive and selfish beings. Nor did others ever feel the need to praise demons for anything. The only way he could think of answering that was with one simple truth. "Demons don't compliment each other." Ever. And not in anything.

"Well, maybe they should."

Maybe she was right. Maybe they should. If they did, perhaps there'd be less animosity between demons, more kinship, but that was a pipe dream. "If a demon ever complimented another demon, it would sound like, 'The way you cracked that skull was cold-blooded, bro.' Although, they wouldn't say 'bro.'"

"Really? Because I think there's a lot of things someone could compliment a demon about. Like..." She trailed a fingertip along one of his horns. "...how big your horns are." She skimmed the back of her finger along the side of his neck, making him still. "Or how gorgeous your skin tone is." She grasped his bicep. "Or how strong you are." She leaned down and inhaled his scent, surprising him. "Or how you smell so amazing…spicy but sweet."

He cleared his throat. "Stop, baby doll. You're making me blush."

"Am I really?" She peeked around his shoulder, and he knew she was catching sight of the flush of his skin stretching from the side of his nose to his temple. Smiling, she pressed a kiss to his cheek. "You're such an adorable demon, Thatch."

"There's no such thing as an adorable demon."

"Lies. Demon babies are adorable. Demon children, too. And I'm sure there are adorable demon ladies."

Okay, so she had him there. He thought of his petite but feisty grandmother. "My demon grandmother, on my mother's side, is pretty adorable, but I'm not." He was far too big.

"Being adorable doesn't always have to do with looks, Thatch. You have such a teddy bear personality. You're like a marshmallow demon."

He roared with laughter. "I'm a marshmallow demon?" Should he turn in his demon card?

She scratched her nails along his head and set to work braiding close to his scalp. "That's right. You're a soft gooey demon. Like a marshmallow."

"Only you could get away with calling me that."

"How much will you let me get away with?"

"Anything and everything, baby doll."

"Could I give you a manicure?"

“Paint my nails, baby.”

“Get you to wear pink?”

“I’ll wear pink from head to foot.”

“Cut your hair?”

“Find scissors.”

“Mm. No.” She worked her fingers through his hair. “I could never cut your hair. Trim it, maybe, but I like it long.”

He shivered as she stroked his scalp and goosebumps stole his body.

“Does that feel good?” she asked.

Better than he could explain. “No one else has ever done my hair. Not as an adult. My mother braided my hair as a child, before she taught me. I’m not used to feeling someone else braiding my hair. I like it.”

“I like making you shiver.”

He stiffened. Sure, he’d been hit on, come-ons had been aimed at him, and creatures attempted to flirt with him, but he never engaged. That didn’t mean he was immune. He wasn’t a virgin, but he’d never had someone as sweet as Aster say anything like that to him. “Baby doll, that sounded dirty.”

“I guess it was supposed to.”

He sucked in a breath. She was going to have him doing things he shouldn’t, like carrying her off to have his way with her. Except, he couldn’t do that. Yes, they’d done some wonderful things, but he yearned to do far more.

She continued to braid his hair, creating three neat rows, starting by his ear, from hairline to the tips of his hair. After she finished those three, she stepped around him to his other side and repeated the process. She’d just finished the third braid on the right side of his head when her alarm went off. "I have to go back. Remove the needles. I don't want Case to pass out from giving Paisley too much blood."

"That's unlikely to happen."

"Still." She fixed his hair along his back. "Stay here. I'm not done."

"I'll be right here when you return."

And he was right there when she returned.

Whatever joy braiding his hair had brought her had been wiped away in the few minutes she'd been gone. "Paisley?" he asked.

"She's asleep. And Case looks…hurt. I think Case blames himself for this, but it's not his fault. Or hers. I took out Case's needle, but I'm giving him a moment so the blood left in the tubing will go to Paisley. I swear he wasn't going to allow me to remove his needle just now."

Thatch nodded. "I get it. I'd do anything for you, too. I'd give you all my blood. Every last drop."

She gaped. "Thatch…"

He drew her to him, right between his legs. "I mean it. With you, I understand Case's fierce need to protect Paisley. With you, I understand why my demon grandfather risked so much to love my fairy grandmother. I get it, Aster. I'd give you every last drop of my blood."

"I…I need to finish your hair."

He nodded, pushing down the disappointment that she wasn't able to voice how he made her feel, but he had no right to demand it. Not even expect it. But he'd hope for it. Every single day, every fleeting moment, he'd hope for it, as if a demon had any right to hope for a fairy's love and affection.

She stepped behind him, and he closed his eyes when her fingers played with his hair again. Diablo, if he could feel this again, he'd be a blessed demon. If he could hold her in his arms again, sleep beside her again, kiss her again, he'd be a demon blessed unlike any other. Well, aside from his grandfather, who knew a fairy's love…and maybe even Case who had…whatever he had with Paisley, part fairy. Thatch just wanted to be half as lucky as his grandfather and Case.

Twisting his hair at the top of his head in a thick braid didn't take her long at all. Soon, she stood in front of him. "You look sexy with your hair like this. Like a warrior demon."

His lips twitched. "I'm glad you're pleased with it."

She fingered one of his braids. "I have to go back. I fear that Case will figure out how to shove the needle back into his vein to give Paisley more blood."

"I wouldn't put it past him."

She was gone only a moment. When she came back, she gave him a nod. "Paisley woke up when I removed the needle in her arm."

"That's good."

She looped her arms around his neck and laid her cheek on his shoulder. "I've never seen her like that. It was scary."

He stroked her back. "I know."

They stayed like that until Paisley's and Case's raised voices reached them.

Aster sighed.

"When those two aren't banging each other, they're arguing," Case said.

"Arguing is one of the things that bonds them."

A knock at Paisley's front door had Aster stepping away from him.

"I should get that," Aster said.

He caught her hand, tugging her to a stop.

"No, I'll get the door."

She hung back by the kitchen entrance while he went to see who was at the door. He checked through the peephole to see Wren standing there. Wren was the demon Case put in charge of the security measures surrounding Paisley's property.

Thatch opened the door fast. "What's going on?"

Wren's dark blue gaze shifted to the side.

Thatch peered back to see Aster there.

Wren lowered his voice. "You should send her to fetch Case so I can tell you without her hearing."

Thatch's spine stiffened. That wasn't good.

"Aster, baby doll, can you get Case for us?"

"Okay." She hurried off, wings fluttering.

The second she was out of earshot, Thatch turned back to Wren. "Tell me."

"I found a dead fairy. Beyond our boundary."

Rage slammed into Thatch.

"Her wings were cut off her back."

Upstairs, Paisley and Case fell silent.

"Come inside," Thatch said. "I'll give Case a heads-up."

He took the stairs two at a time and met Case in the hallway. "It's Wren." That was all he needed to say to convey that the situation was dire.

Case stepped outside with Wren, and Thatch stayed with Aster and Paisley. He hadn't said a word to either of them about what was going on, but he didn't need to. Wren showing up, Case leaving, and now he was sure he exuded worry and fear and anger.

The fact that *another* fairy had been murdered so close to Paisley's house put him on edge. He paced the hall in front of the door.

"Thatch?" Aster tiptoed closer.

He didn't want her getting near any of the windows or doors. Not after the Molotov cocktail. Not after the bullets. Not after two dead fairies.

"It's alright, baby doll, just stay back there."

Paisley took Aster's elbow and tugged Aster back to the staircase where she waited for Case's return. She still looked a bit pale, and her hand shook a little at her side. Was that from the blood loss or from Wren's news? Probably both. He couldn't blame her for either reaction. His own fists were shaking, so he balled his hands tighter, hoping to keep them still.

A few minutes later, Case returned. The rage in Case's golden eyes only made Thatch clench his fists more. Case lifted a hand and called Thatch over to him with a finger. That action, so simple, spoke volumes. Thatch stepped up to Case and took the piece of paper Case held out to him. He unfolded it and read the words that put a fear into him that he'd never felt before.

Aster's next. We'll leave her body where her demon boy-toy will find it.

He whipped toward Aster as the love he had for her put him in a chokehold.

"What's going on?" Paisley demanded and stole the note from his numb fingers.

"Wren found a dead fairy," Case said.

Thatch watched Paisley as she read the words on the note and almost didn't see Aster inching closer. He reached out to snag the note first, but Aster plucked it from Paisley's fingers and read the threat aimed at herself before he could stop her. Her wings shivered and then became immobile with fright as they pressed together. Her beautiful lavender eyes widened and sought his. Terror leeched off her, and every protector instinct rose up in him like a volcano about to erupt.

He dropped to his knees in front of her and grasped her small hands in his, needing her to not only hear his words but feel them coming from his body. "They're not going to touch you, baby doll. On my life, they won't touch you."

"Get her out of here."

His gaze met Paisley's, but she was looking at Case, not him.

"She's not safe here, but she'll be safe at your place, right?"

Case nodded once. "I will have a fucking ring of demons around my mansion. Day and night. No one will get in to hurt her. No one."

The words could've been Thatch's because there was no way in hell he'd allow anyone to harm his precious Aster. Not even Diablo himself would be able to accomplish it.

Aster continued to grip Thatch's hands as she

shook her head and spoke to Paisley. "But I can't leave. I can't leave you here. I just gave you a blood transfusion, for Goddess's sake."

"I'm fine now, but a fairy was killed and your life is being threatened. You can't stay here." Paisley shoved Thatch's shoulder. "Go."

Paisley didn't have to tell him twice.

He shoved to his feet and swept Aster into his arms to take her away from there and straight to safety.

"No, Thatch, please." Despite her words, she clutched him.

Baby Doll, I have to. He couldn't get the words out, though. Still, they echoed inside him like a gong signaling disaster.

Case threw the door open, and Thatch marched toward it.

In his arms, Aster's body shook as she wept. "Please, Thatch, don't. I can't go! Please, please, don't take me away."

But he had to. She was in danger.

The second he stepped through the doorway, his wings erupted from his back, ready to whisk her off to safety.

"Nononono!"

Her pleas clenched around his heart, but they wouldn't halt him. No matter how much he hated her tears, he hated even more that someone wanted her dead.

He rocketed straight up, aiming for Case's mansion.

Aster burrowed herself against him and kept on sobbing into his chest.

He arrived at Case's a moment later and rushed her inside. With the door shut at his back, he carried her into the parlor and embraced her on his lap where she trembled as she cried. Her tears wet his shirt, and it all but killed him. "I'm sorry, baby doll."

"She's my sister," she wept. "I'm all she has, and she's all I have."

"That's not true, baby. She has Case, and you have me."

"But she can't be alone."

He slid his hand under her hair and cupped the back of her neck. "She won't be alone. Case will be with her."

"But if she needs healing—" She let out a sob.

"Then Case will bring her here or come and get you. He won't let anything happen to her, and I'm not going to let anything happen to you."

His words only made her cry harder. At a loss for how to comfort a grieving fairy, he simply held her and caressed her back in calming circles.

Several minutes later, he heard the front door open, and Case stepped inside the parlor.

Aster swiped her hands over her cheeks. "What are you doing here? You should be with Paisley."

"She's going to the faye faction to take care of the fairy. I can't go there with her. I'm not welcome."

She glanced at Thatch and then looked to Case again. "You don't know that."

He gave her a small smile. "I appreciate that *you* like me, cutie pie, but not all fairies do. I'm not the teddy bear that Thatch is."

Thatch sighed, but the way Aster cuddled against

him, well, he realized there was nothing wrong with being called a teddy bear when you had a lovely fairy snuggling against you as if you really were one.

"They will like you eventually," she said to Case. "But I should be helping Paisley. I should be at the faye faction."

"You are exactly where you need to be." Case nudged his chin forward. "In Thatch's arms."

At Case's words, Thatch's arms flexed around her. Yes, in his arms was exactly where she belonged.

"We have to protect you now, cutie pie, and we're going to take that job seriously. Every demon here is going to protect you with their lives. Including me." His gaze met Thatch's, and he gave a small nod, vowing to Thatch that he'd protect Aster because she was important to Case, too. She was family. "Thatch will show you to your room and get you whatever you need so you can feel at home, because, for the time being, this *is* your home." Case reached out and tweaked Aster's chin with a brotherly affection. "And then tonight, we'll have a proper fairy feast. With all the fruits and vegetables you could want."

She smiled.

"I'll be off. I'm sending demons to surround the faye faction. I'll be back later. The two of you have the mansion."

Thatch glared at Case's smirk before he stepped out of sight.

The front door opened and closed again.

"Thatch…"

He kissed Aster on the top of her head.

"Bring me to my room."

Thatch carried Aster up the stairs to the room across from his, although every part of him wanted to bring her into his room, into his bed.

11

Pink Lace Panties

Thatch opened the door to a room with flowered wallpaper and a canopy bed with gauzy curtains. It was pretty, but not even a pretty bed would change the fact that she wasn't home or that a fairy had died or that someone wanted to do the same to her. Thatch set her on the edge of the bed, between two sheer blue curtains. She reached out to touch the material. "It's pretty."

"This room belonged to a demon princess centuries ago. They said she was beautiful." He traced her jaw with the tip of his finger. "But I doubt she was half as beautiful as you."

She scooted back onto the mattress. "I'm tired."

"It was a long morning."

She glanced at the stacked pillows. "Will you lie down with me?"

"I can't fit on this bed."

"Then we'll break it."

Thatch jolted at her words.

She offered a small laugh. "I didn't mean like that." Then she reached up, gripped a handful of the sheer curtains, and tugged. The material ripped from the canopy and floated down to her. She grabbed the curtains on the other side of her and tore those down, too. Sure, they'd been pretty, but what was a pretty bed if you couldn't share it with the demon you loved? So, she balled the material up and chucked it onto the floor. "You can climb on now, and if the bed breaks, it breaks. We could always have another one built. One for us."

Thatch's Adam's apple bobbed. "I could build it for us."

She crawled backward to the center of the bed. "Then we won't really need this one, now will we?"

"I suppose not." And he approached.

When he placed a knee on the bed, it creaked.

When he knelt on it with both knees, it groaned.

He made his way to her, wrapped his arms around her, and laid down on the mattress with her tucked close to his body.

The bed held.

She snuggled against him.

"Rest, baby doll. I've got you."

And because she knew he did, and she trusted him totally, she was able to drift off to sleep.

Two hours later, she woke, and Paisley still wasn't there.

A feast of every fruit and vegetable imaginable was prepared by Case's chefs, and the three of them ate it. The only one missing was Paisley. She never showed up for dinner. She never even sent word.

Aster asked Case if he should go and check on Paisley, but he said Paisley told him she'd come when she was finished.

"She must not be finished yet," Case said. "If she doesn't come tonight, I'll check in on her in the morning."

The two demons did what they could to keep her mind off the tragedy of the day, the fear that she'd be next, and worrying about Paisley by teaching her how to play poker. Case laughed good and loud when she won three hands in a row.

"Alright," Case said. "Get her out of here before she embarrasses me further. I can't let the Enchanted Hierarchy find out that a fairy cleaned me out of my fortune under my own roof."

"Oh, but I wouldn't have taken *all* of your money," she teased.

Case grinned. "She's a gem, Thatch. You could learn a thing or two from her."

"I never claimed to be a pro poker player."

Thatch's grumble made her giggle, but even beneath that distraction…she knew…she remembered. Nothing could get her to forget why she was there.

But where was Paisley?

Thatch escorted her back to her bedroom to tuck her into bed, or so she hoped, but he paused at the door. "I should probably go to Paisley's in the morning to grab you some clothes. You won't have anything to wear tomorrow, and you don't have anything to wear to bed."

Beside the bed, Aster faced him. "That's okay." She reached behind her and pulled down the zipper to her dress. It slid down her body and piled into a puff of fabric around her feet. Underneath, all she wore were her pink lace panties. "I can go to bed like this."

Thatch stilled. His gaze latched onto her and didn't flick away. His chest rose and fell as he breathed deeply. Suddenly, he jerked toward the opened bedroom door. He sprang in front of the opening, grabbed the door, and secured it into place. A second later, he whipped around, took two long strides, and lifted her clear off her feet. With a hand at the back of her head, he kissed her with a fierceness that stole her breath and had her entire body tingling with urges.

She wrapped her legs around his waist and tugged her body as close to him as possible. When she felt the button of his pants scrape against her crotch, igniting her pussy with awareness, she gasped into his kiss. She couldn't stop from rolling her hips forward, hoping to repeat the sensation. "Thatch."

Saying his name snapped whatever control he must've had, because he was crawling onto the bed, with her wrapped around him. The frame creaked beneath their weight. When he stretched out on the mattress, his hands grasped her hips, and he pulled her down, right over the bulge in his pants. "Do you feel that, baby?"

Biting her bottom lip, she nodded.

"I want you to rub yourself against my erection. Don't stop until you come."

Palms pressed to his chest, she began to grind against that magnificent bulge. The friction was glorious. She'd never felt anything like it, had never had the desire to dry hump anything. Until Thatch. And everything they did together was so new and so stunning in pleasure that she wasn't sure what she'd do if one day the pleasure became too much. What would it feel like to have his cock pumping deep inside her? She wasn't sure she'd ever find out, but she could imagine it. While rubbing her covered pussy over his restrained cock, she vibrated with the urge to unzip his pants, nudge her panties to the side, and fill herself with him. He claimed doing that would hurt her, but how could accepting a part of a demon who she loved into herself hurt her? This demon who cared for her so much. This demon who was devoted to her in every way. This demon who adored her. This demon who she wanted to be with in every way.

A moan floated past her lips.

Her pussy was tingling, her clit singing, her body trembling.

She ground against his erection faster.

His fingertips dug into the fleshiest part of her hips, and he groaned while holding onto her. She liked knowing she could do that, make such a large demon groan with needs. His hips jutted off the bed. When his erection bumped into her pussy, she moaned with him. Sensations vibrated up her clitoris gland like a bell tolling.

She shifted her hands to his shoulders to use him as her anchor. Head bent, she ground against him quick as a whip but also deep and thorough. It was becoming too much, though, as it usually did when she masturbated. And this wasn't any different than those times. She was essentially using Thatch as a giant sex toy, and she didn't think she could do what he'd requested—rub herself against him until she came. What she did felt so overwhelming that she slowed her movements before her hips shuddered to a stop entirely.

"What's wrong, baby doll?"

"I…I don't think I can."

His brows furrowed, and he caressed her sides with the tenderest of touches. "Why not?"

"Remember when I told you I could never get myself there? That I'd never orgasmed by myself before?"

He nodded.

"I think I need help. Your help. I can't do it alone. I need you to push me over the brink."

He inhaled. "Then get ready to fall."

In a swift motion, he had her on her back beneath him with the bulge of his cock firmly pressed between her legs. He rubbed his erection over her covered pussy. She couldn't stop from digging her nails into his solid back. She couldn't stop her legs from trembling. She couldn't stop her eyes from rolling back. And because *he* didn't stop, she couldn't halt the orgasm that erupted from every nerve ending in her clitoris and vulva.

As she came down from the high of her orgasm, he kissed her slowly. Then he shifted to the side and tucked her against his body. “Goodnight, Aster.”

“Night, Thatch.” And she drifted off to a peaceful sleep.

She dreamed so soundlessly in his arms that she slept past when she usually woke up and only came to when a loud crash jolted her awake.

Thatch bolted upright.

“What was that?” she asked.

More crashing sounds.

Thatch jumped to his feet.

Aster gathered her blanket to her chest. “Is the mansion under attack?”

“I don’t know. Stay here.” He secured the door behind him.

Banging noises grew louder.

She tugged on her discarded dress, and even though Thatch had told her to stay in her room, she couldn’t do that. Couldn’t not find out what was going on. Couldn’t not be there with Thatch. If the mansion was being attacked, she’d help defend it.

Bag of spikes and dart in hand, she raced down the stairs and followed the noises to the parlor to find not members of an enemy faction, but Case. He stood in the middle of the room’s carnage with a mahogany chair leg gripped in his hands. Thatch had him in a headlock so tight it looked like he aimed to make Case pass out in order to stop him, but Case broke free and slammed the chair leg into Thatch’s head. She gasped and flinched backward as the wood fell apart in Case’s hands from the impact of the hit. Thankfully, Thatch was still standing, but Case appeared to want to keep on going and attack his best friend. She leapt forward.

"Case!"

He jerked as if he'd collided into a wall. His golden gaze landed on her. He was breathing hard.

"What's going on?"

He sucked in a breath. "Paisley left."

Aster frowned. "What?"

"She. Fucking. Left." He held out a crumpled piece of paper to her.

She took it and read Paisley's words.

Case,

I can't do this anymore. I know we had an agreement. One that I take seriously. We promised not to leave without talking to the other first. Not to end things on a whim. Not unless there was true betrayal or mutual agreement. Or one of us did something against our factions. I received damning evidence that you have been behind the attempts on my life this entire time. I can't ignore that. I can't forgive that. I'm sorry. It's over. I'm leaving. Don't try to find me.

Paisley

Not a single word Aster read made sense, and she

told Case that, tried to explain that Paisley wouldn't have left without saying anything to her. Paisley wouldn't have done that. They'd been best friends for too long, told each other everything. Their friendship was important, and so were promises. Leaving without a word wasn't like Paisley.

"I found this, too."

Aster stared at the diamond-encrusted paisley that dangled from Case's hand. The only time she'd ever seen that necklace off Paisley's neck was when Paisley's mom had given it to her. It'd been nestled in a suede box at the time. Since then, it'd always been there whenever Aster saw her. No matter how late or how early.

She told Case that, too, but he didn't seem to believe her.

"What do you think?" he asked Thatch.

"Paisley wouldn't have left without telling Aster. I'm confident about that."

Aster nodded.

Case turned back to Aster. "If she had really left, she would've left someone in charge. I'd think she'd leave you in charge of the faye faction."

They'd discussed it several times, long before Paisley was coronated. She knew Paisley's wishes, that she'd take over and rule the faye faction if anything were to happen to her. But that was never supposed to happen.

She lifted a slender shoulder. "Maybe…maybe she left me a note in my bedroom?"

"We'll check."

She didn't believe Paisley wouldn't have discussed

her plans before leaving, made sure Aster was okay with her decision and ready to take on such an important role. Nor did she think Paisley would desert the faye faction in their time of need, when another fairy had shown up dead.

Aster's eyes widened. "If Paisley is gone…" She shook her head. "…no." She couldn't go there. Wouldn't.

"What is it?"

She met Case's eye. "The dead fairy. I don't believe she'd leave one of our own in the woods to decompose without a proper burial ceremony." But since Paisley had left, it fell to Aster. "I'm sorry, Case, but I need to check on that first."

"The three of us will. Thatch."

Thatch swept Aster into his arms before she could even blink. "Already got her covered."

He stepped outside behind Case. Before launching into the air, he laid his hand to the back of her head. While he flew toward Paisley's, she closed her eyes to enjoy his closeness, his warmth, his scent. She lifted her head closer to his neck and kissed the side of his throat.

His chest expanded against her. He lowered his head to say into her ear, "Not while I'm flying, baby doll."

"Sorry."

A moment later, they landed in the woods where Wren stood guard near a body covered by a flower-print blanket. The fact Wren had done that touched her, but the fairy shouldn't have been there. Paisley should've taken care of her. "Paisley wouldn't have left her. She wouldn't have done that." She would've started the burial rites to make sure the fairy was put to rest respectfully and with honor.

"Take Aster to the faye faction," Case said to Thatch. Then his gaze met Aster's. "Bring Paisley's council here to take care of this fairy. I'll stay here."

She nodded, and Thatch picked her up again. He carried her to the faye faction and set her on her feet in front of the main house.

Mum met them with a smile. "Hello, you two. What a pleasant surprise."

Aster sighed. "Unfortunately, we're not here for a pleasant visit.

12

They led Paisley's faye council members back to the fairy in the woods. While they wrapped the fairy, Thatch stood guard with Wren. The fairies took great care covering the fairy from head to toe and folding a blanket over her wings. One of the fairies lifted the wings off the ground.

"Thatch?" Mum looked up at him. "We could use your help bringing her back."

"Of course." He lifted her gently into his arms, not liking how stiff she was or that her size and weight reminded him of Aster. He never wanted to feel Aster like this in his arms. Ever. His gaze went to Aster and then to Wren. "Protect her with your life."

Wren dipped his chin in silent acknowledgement.

Thatch flew the fairy back to the faye faction and carried her into the main house where he laid her on a table.

"Thank you, Thatch." Mum touched his arm. "We've got it from here."

"Aster and I will come back later."

Mum nodded.

He found Case with Aster and Wren when he returned. Without a word, he and Case followed Aster into the house so they could look for another letter from Paisley, but there wasn't one. They gathered in the parlor to discuss where she would've gone, and the consensus was that she would've sought out Jude, Paisley's godfather and the centaur king.

Aster contacted him on her mobile phone. "Jude, it's Aster. Is Paisley there? No, Paisley's gone. I mean she left. We don't know where she went. She left a note. It said she was leaving because"—she paused and gave Case an apologetic look for the next words that were going to come out of her mouth—"because she got evidence that Case was behind the attempts on her life." She shook her head vehemently. "No, Jude, he wouldn't do that." She bit her lip. "We're…we're at Paisley's." Her gaze flicked back to Case. "Yes, Case, too. Jude? Hello?" She lowered her phone. "He hung up. I think he's coming." She slipped her phone back into her purse. "He doesn't sound very happy."

"I imagine not." Case sat on the love seat. "When he gets here, point him in my direction."

Thatch crossed his arms, not thrilled with the fact

that Case appeared ready to take a beating even though he didn't deserve one. The problem was, Case probably thought he did deserve it. Thatch supposed he could understand that. If something happened to Aster, or if she ran away, if she chose to never see or speak to Thatch again… Yeah, he'd be one-hundred percent at fault regardless of what would've led to those outcomes.

A short time later, a fist pounded on the front door.

Thatch went to it, fully prepared to stop Jude from hitting Case if it meant taking the first fist or hoof himself. He opened the door to Jude's pissed-off glare.

"Move."

Thatch let him enter but stayed by his side so he could step in if necessary.

Jude made his way into the parlor with a click of hooves on tile and pointed at Case. "What the hell did you do to my goddaughter, you demonic son-of-a-bitch?"

So much for being friends. But Thatch understood it. Paisley was Jude's family. He'd known her all her life. She wasn't just a goddaughter to Jude, but like a *real* daughter. He'd kill for her. As would Case, who was oddly calm as he stood and offered Jude one good hit.

Aster scrambled between them, putting her hands up as barricades. "He didn't do anything. It's a lie. It's all lies."

"Then why would Paisley believe it?"

Case lifted his hands. Not in surrender but in a show of confusion and exasperation. "I don't know. I'd think she'd know me a little by now, but she apparently still thinks the worst of me."

Jude crossed his arms. "If she's not here, and she's not with me, then where is she?"

Case shrugged. "We were hoping you'd know."

"I don't. So, she really left?"

Case didn't answer but gave Paisley's note to Jude.

Jude lowered it. "What damning evidence is she talking about?"

"There is no evidence. If there is, someone faked it. I swear to you, I swear to Paisley, I swear to Aster, the most innocent person I fucking know, I swear to Diablo himself, that I never did anything to put her in harm's way, and I didn't kill a single fairy. Someone is framing me, just like they did when they burned my brand into Paisley's lawn."

And if anyone doubted Case's words or what he felt for Paisley or even Aster in that moment, then they weren't paying attention.

Jude's slow nod told Thatch that he could see it, hear it, sense it…everything that Paisley and Aster meant to Case. "Until we find out the truth, let's keep this quiet. We'll wait to see if Paisley comes back. If she doesn't show up for the next meeting, we'll tell the other faction leaders then."

"And until then, what do we do?"

"Hope she comes back."

Thatch glanced at Aster as she stared at the floor. She didn't appear to have any hope that her best friend would return. A hopeless fairy wasn't natural. Fairies and elves were full of hope, but Aster had been through a lot. A death threat and her best friend disappearing might just be too much even for a fairy to keep her faith.

"Let's go back to my place," Case said. "Maybe we can figure out where she went or how to look for her."

And Aster would be safer there, too. Thatch liked that plan.

Case took a step to leave.

Thatch turned to follow suit, and all he saw was a blur of black. Silas, Paisley's vampire uncle, had Case pinned to the wall, in a spiderweb of cracked plaster.

"What the fuck did you do?" Silas shouted, with a hand around Case's throat. "What did you do to Paisley?!"

Before Thatch could make a move, Case rammed a fist into Silas's stomach and then his face.

Silas dropped to the floor.

Case stood over him. "I didn't do a fucking thing!"

Silas attempted to get to his feet, but Jude stopped him with a hoof to his chest, keeping him flat against the floor while Case shouted his frustrations.

"I am sick of everyone thinking I did something to Paisley. I didn't do a damn thing but care about her."

Thatch and Aster exchanged looks.

A little knowing smile tugged at Aster's lips. They'd long figured out that Case and Paisley cared for each other. It was Case and Paisley who'd taken longer to figure it out.

Silas's mocking laughter pulled their attentions. "A sex demon cares about someone?"

Oh no the bastard didn't.

Even Aster looked ready to hurt Silas for that.

Case's hands balled into fists at his sides. "I will fuck you up and dump your ass outside in the sun to burn to a crisp. Try me."

The sneer on Silas's face was begging to get wiped off by a fist or hoof. "Believe Paisley will forgive you for that?"

"Maybe it'll be enough to get her to come back." And in the next second, Case was making his move to give Silas that well-deserved beating.

But Thatch wasn't expecting how quick Aster was. She blocked Case and stuck her hands between demon and vampire. "Stop, stop, stop! This isn't helping. Paisley wouldn't want us fighting."

"Then maybe she shouldn't have fucking left," Case snapped.

Aster flinched at his anger, even if it wasn't really toward her.

"She left because of you," Silas shouted.

"What the hell do you even know about it? About Paisley and me? Nothing!"

"I know what she wrote me."

Thatch blinked. *What*?

Aster approached Silas. "She gave you a letter?"

"I found it at my door."

Aster's wings fluttered—a flicker of hope. "What did it say?"

Silas turned his head to glare at Jude. "Get your filthy hoof off me."

Bigoted bastard.

Jude allowed Silas to shove to his feet.

Silas tugged a folded piece of paper from his pocket and shoved it at Aster with more aggression than necessary. "Read it yourself."

Aster took it as if it were delicate, made of

something that'd crumble, like soft, gray ash. She unfolded the letter and read it from beginning to end. Then she handed it to Case so he could read Paisley's words.

After Case finished, he lowered the note down to Paisley's line of sight. "Does that look like a tear?"

Aster nodded. "It does. If she was upset, there might've been tears."

Silas surged forward. "And what the fuck did you do to make my niece cry and leave?"

Aster blocked him with her tiny body. "You don't understand. Case didn't do anything."

Case faced Thatch. "Pick up your beautiful fairy and get her out of the way. I don't want her hurt. If Silas wants to feel more pain, I'll give it to him."

That right there revealed that Case cared about Aster. He didn't like the thought of her getting hurt or putting herself between him and a vampire. And neither did Thatch. He plucked Aster off her feet and set her on the floor at his side. Now he could block her with his own body or hold her back if he needed to.

Silas advanced on Case.

Jude stepped up now to get between them. "Aster's right. Case didn't have anything to do with why Paisley left."

"Her note says he does."

Aster tried to take a step, but Thatch halted her. "She was lied to."

"By whom?"

"We don't know."

"Convenient. If Paisley says she can't trust Case, then I can't trust him."

"Fine," Case seethed. "Don't trust me. I don't care what *you* think of me. I care what *she* thinks of me, and I will prove that whatever someone told her is a lie. If you care about your niece, you'll call a truce with me and help."

Silas didn't do anything for a moment but glare at Case. Then he seemed to relent. "I suppose for my niece I can call a temporary truce, but don't think I'm going to shake your hand."

"Yeah, I'm not fucking touching you unless I'm bruising you." Case looked left and right. "How the hell did you get in here?"

Thatch looked, too. Windows were intact and filtering in sunlight. The front door was shut. There was no way for a full-blown vampire to make it into Paisley's house without getting at least third-degree burns.

"The underground tunnel."

Silas's answer had Case whirling toward Aster. "What fucking underground tunnel?"

Aster's grimace told Thatch that what she was about to say, Case wouldn't like. "Um…the underground tunnel that goes from Paisley's house to the vamprye faction. She…she never told you about it?"

Hell, Thatch didn't like it. What if someone had used it while he was there protecting Aster? Or during the brief times when they were in Paisley's house alone? He wouldn't have known it. They could've snuck up on him, killed him before he even realized intruders were in the house, and then done Diablo-only-knows-what to Aster and Paisley. And Aster had never told him. They'd have a conversation about that later.

"Show me," Case demanded.

Aster led them to the basement and behind a shelf that hid a tunnel. They walked the winding path underground in silence for several minutes before Case asked the same question Thatch wondered.

"What was this tunnel used for?"

"It's an escape route for the royal family," Silas said. "And, in the event of war, the entire vamprye faction could use it to flee an ambush. Like from the daemon faction."

Case spun on his heel.

Thatch caught him with a hand to his shoulder to keep him from attacking. "Don't engage."

Clenching his jaw, Case continued on. "Who else knows about this?"

"Just Paisley's council."

"I'll want their names."

"Why?"

Thatch knew why without Case even having to say it.

"Because one of them could've been behind her assassination attempts."

"What does that even matter now? She's gone. Because of you. She believes you're the one behind the attempts on her life."

At the same time as Case about-faced, Thatch dodged to the side, giving him full access to Silas to do whatever he pleased.

"I will find out the truth, and you'll get out of my fucking way so I can," Case growled. "If you interfere in any way, I will break you."

Silas smirked. "And start a war with the vampyre faction?"

Case didn't say more but turned back around.

At the end of the tunnel, Silas went home and the rest of them returned to Paisley's. Their trek down there had been futile. If Paisley had used it, she hadn't left behind any proof. Not even a footprint because of the cobblestone. Which meant there was also no evidence that anyone else had snuck through the tunnel. Not even Silas, who had just used it.

In Paisley's parlor, Aster slipped her hand in his.

Jude laid a supportive hand on her shoulder.

And the three of them stared at Case. They did nothing but that. Thatch had never seen Case so lost before. Even in the middle of somewhere they all knew.

Finally, Case turned. "I'm leaving."

The front door slammed behind him.

Now it was the three of them, standing there. Lost.

Jude squeezed Aster's shoulder. "I'll go to my faction. Make sure she hasn't turned up there while I was gone."

Aster nodded.

Then it was just him and Aster.

"I should pack my things, and we should go, too. I need to be at the faye faction."

"Of course." He watched her fold dresses and slips and nightgowns into a suitcase and top it off with the prettiest panty and bra sets he'd ever seen. "Can you model those for me later?"

She lifted a ruffled, lacy article that looked more like a tube top with little cap sleeves than a bra. "This?"

"All of it."

Her cheeks brightened. “I just might.” She zipped the suitcase.

“I’ve got that.” He lifted the suitcase off her bed.

“You just want to be close to my panties.”

He leaned down to whisper in her ear. “If I wanted to get close to your panties, I’d choose the ones you’re wearing.”

Her small hand pushed against his abs. “Ssh.”

He shifted back. “Did you just hush me in private?”

“Yes, because I’m blushing, and if you keep up like this, I’ll be wet *and* blushing, and I can’t be either in front of Mum.”

He grinned. “Alright, baby doll. I’ll stop.” Then he bent down, hooked an arm under her lovely butt, and lifted her off her feet. “To the faye faction?”

She nodded.

At the faye faction, he dug the fairy’s grave and cleaned up her burial site while Aster wove wicker for the casket and braided daisies for the fairy ring. He was covered in dirt when he sat on the steps in front of the main house. As a breeze swept over him, cooling the sweat on his arms, he rubbed his hands to remove the dirt smudges. The last thing he wanted was to soil Aster’s pretty dress. He sighed and lowered his hands; the dirt wasn’t going anywhere.

Tiny white petals rained down on him.

He smiled when Aster joined him on the step. A literal fairy shedding flower petals wherever she went. He was far too lucky of a demon to have a fairy he could kiss whenever he wanted.

Her hand slipped against his palm, and her fingers

twined with his. "We're done. We'll lay her to rest tomorrow."

Nodding, Thatch lifted her hand and pressed a kiss to it. "This is the second time I've had to dig a grave for a fairy." His thumb grazed her knuckles. "I don't like it. Each time, I think about you in that hole, in one of those little wicker coffins, and—" He shook his head. "I can't. I can't picture you dead and buried. I refuse to let anyone hurt you. I refuse to lose you."

She rose onto her knees and pressed a kiss to his cheek. "You won't lose me. I'm not going anywhere. Except wherever you go."

He swooped her around until she was stretched out over his lap, and he kissed her so slow and deep that he sank into the kiss, thoroughly losing himself in it. Their kiss took him away from the tragedy of a fairy's murder and the confusion over Paisley's disappearance. For a moment, it was just the two of them, locked in a passionate embrace. But then it was suddenly all the fairies who'd been taking part of the funeral preparations as they broke out in applause.

Aster pulled away and covered her face with her hands. "Oh my Goddess, are they all watching?"

Two young fairies were giggling, a group of fairy women were fanning themselves, and in the middle of it all, Mum was looking like a proud mama, gushing to the other fairies.

"Yeah, they are."

She groaned.

Thatch laughed. "I'll get you out of here." He stood with her in his arms.

A chorus of sighs filled the air as the fairies

swooned.

Aster whacked him in the shoulder. “Stop being so sexy.”

“I’m just doing what I usually do.”

“Which is sexy.”

“Well, I’m not going to stop protecting you or carrying you, so your fairy friends will have to get over it.” He summoned his wings and flew to Case’s mansion. There was no sign of Case on the grounds or the first floor. The hall to the second floor was empty, too. With Paisley gone, Case could be anywhere. He could even be out there somewhere searching for Paisley. Thatch wouldn’t put it past him.

“Case could be anywhere.”

Aster nodded.

“I’m going to shower.”

Aster’s gaze trailed down his body.

He grinned. “If I weren’t this dirty, I’d be asking you if you’d like a shower for two.” He pinched her chin as her cheeks flushed. “Next time, baby doll.”

He showered and dressed in clean clothes. Then he and Aster cooked pasta together and ate it while watching *Barbie* the movie, which Thatch was surprised to find he enjoyed, although he could never admit that in the presence of another demon. Only for Aster would he watch a rom-com. Especially if it meant seeing her smile and hearing her laughter.

After the movie ended, she went off to soak in a bath, another thing that he promised himself they’d share the next time. In his room, he was getting out sweatpants from a drawer and wondering if he would be sleeping in his bed or Aster’s that night. Was it wrong of him to assume that they'd be sleeping together at all? Because he liked the idea of having her in his arms at night. He picked up a pair of dark gray sweats and turned to find Aster standing in the doorway wearing a pink cotton nightgown. She'd look adorably sweet if it weren't for the tears in her eyes.

He set the sweatpants aside. "What's wrong?"

She lifted her hands and then let them fall to her sides. "Everything. Another fairy is dead. Paisley is gone. Case is wrecked." She shook her head. "I'm really, really sad." A tear plunged down her cheek, punctuating her words.

Heart tearing for her, he went to her, drew her to him, and kissed her forehead. "You can cry as much as you need to. I've got you."

She did cry.

And he held her until she ran out of tears.

13

Pride & Prejudice

Thatch attended another funeral with her. They'd gone to more funerals than dates. This wasn't how things were supposed to go, but Aster was happy to have him there standing beside her, holding her hand, being her rock, her tower, her everything. With another fairy in the ground, the earth covering the wicker casket, and Paisley's absence noticed and felt by all, a gloom fell over the faye faction. After a fairy is laid to rest, there was usually food and drink and music to celebrate the fairy's life. They did their best to honor this fairy killed in a gruesome manner, but it was hard when they could very well be here in another week, doing it all again. And next time, it might be Aster in the ground, tucked inside a wicker casket, getting earth piled on top of her.

As flutes and harps played a pretty melody, Thatch and Aster strolled away from the celebration of life. Thatch's thumb swept over her knuckles. Back and forth. Back and forth. Neither of them said anything until they were far from the others and the tune on the breeze was faint.

"Aster, why didn't you tell me about the tunnel?"

She looked up at Thatch, confused by his question. "What?"

"The tunnel under Paisley's house. Why didn't you tell me about it?"

"I…" She frowned. His question, the softness of his voice, the way he didn't look at her, it was clear that he thought she'd kept that information from him intentionally, but nothing could be further from the truth. "I didn't keep it from you or not tell you on purpose."

And because he still wouldn't look at her, she scurried around him, flattened her hands to his abs, and pushed him to a standstill. "I swear, Thatch. The tunnel was never my business, so I never thought of it." He frowned at her with his brows furrowed. "Honestly, I should've. I should've thought of it and realized it was a potential threat, but if Paisley didn't think so, then I…" She stared up at him, desperate for him to forgive her. "I'm sorry."

He laid a hand to her cheek. "It's okay."

She closed her eyes and turned her face into his

palm.

His lips grazed against her forehead. "The thought that something could've happened to you because I didn't know about that damn tunnel…"

She held his waist. "I'm sorry."

"Ssh." He tilted her head back with his fingers at her chin and laid his lips against hers. "I know. I know, baby doll. You're just so precious to me. Thinking about what could've happened if someone had discovered that tunnel and found you there in Paisley's house. Even if I'd been there, they still could've gotten to you. And that—" His hands suddenly yanked her onto tiptoe, and he crushed his mouth to hers.

She latched onto him and kissed him back with equal passion. The kiss was so consuming, so fulfilling, so everything that her wings fluttered rapidly with the power of it. His tongue delved into her mouth, sliding like satin against hers. He growled at the back of his throat, and she moaned in response.

After a moment, though, Thatch pulled back, chuckling.

"Baby doll, you're floating again."

Her wings had beat so fast that she had risen off the ground and hovered a few inches higher than Thatch so that he was now looking up at her. "Sorry."

Shaking his head, he hooked an arm around her and held her close. "Don't ever be sorry for floating off the ground because of one of our kisses. I want you to float. I want you to go weak. I want you to forget your name."

She smiled. "Then keep kissing me, because I remember my name."

His hand curled around the back of her neck, and he deepened the kiss.

She sighed and became languid in his arms.

"There you go," he muttered against her mouth.

"Take me home. I mean, to Case's."

"Alright." His wings smacked the air gently, and the wind swooped around her as he flew back to Case's, with her tucked close.

When they entered Case's mansion, he was there, bottle of whiskey and glass in one hand, Paisley's necklace dangling from the other. He was heading toward the stairs to, she imagined, drink himself unconscious.

Thatch set Aster on her feet, and she rushed after Case as he took a couple of steps up the staircase. "Wait," she called after him while dipping her fingers into the satchel at her waist.

His shoulders lowered. A sigh left him, and he turned.

She stood at the foot of the stairs and held up her hand. Between her thumb and forefinger, she pinched the stem of a daisy. She'd saved it for him, thinking that the pretty yellow head and white petals would make him smile. That was all she wanted—to see Case smile again.

Except, there was a frown on his face as he stuffed Paisley's necklace into his pocket and took the daisy from her. "What is this?"

"It's—" She fiddled with her fingers. "It's a flower. I thought…I thought it might make you happy, but I guess that's silly. A flower couldn't possibly make you happy."

The corner of his mouth tilted up slowly. "But the sweetest fairy in existence giving me a flower can make me happy. Thank you, cutie pie. I'll cherish this." And he carried the daisy upstairs with the bottle of whiskey.

Thatch ran a hand down Aster's hair. "I think only one thing…one person…will get Case out of this."

Now she was the one sighing. "Paisley."

"Yeah."

"I miss her, too."

"I know you do."

"I'm unhappy, too." Maybe she wasn't as unhappy as Case, because the poor demon was shattered and holding himself together with whiskey and the chain of Paisley's necklace. But she was grieving her best friend's absence nonetheless. The only reason she wasn't falling to pieces was because of Thatch. "But when I'm with you, I'm not unhappy anymore."

He drew her to him. "Fortunately, I'll always be with you, and I'll do whatever I can to lift your spirits."

And he genuinely did everything he could to lift Aster's spirits in the weeks following Paisley's disappearance, including asking Case if she could plant a small garden on his property, to which Case had agreed. In return, she did her best to not seem so unhappy. So, when he fetched the DVD of *Pride & Prejudice* from Paisley's house in an effort to cheer her up, she pasted on a smile and took a place on Case's couch to watch the film with Thatch. He slipped the disc into the device before sitting next to her and tucking her close. She snuggled in, determined to have a good time with Thatch.

The piano's first notes rang out. When they picked

up to play the iconic opening number, Thatch sucked in a quick intake of breath.

She smiled and let herself calm to the music, safe in his warm embrace.

The song faded, and he said, "Paisley was right. The music is magickal."

"You'll have to tell her that if she comes back."

"When," he corrected and kissed her temple.

Despite her lapse, she ended up having a fun time witnessing Thatch experience the film for the first time. His commentary throughout delighted her.

"What's wrong with Miss Lucas?" he asked when Mrs. Bennett was putting the poor girl's looks down in front of the newcomers. "She's pretty, kind, has a great personality, and is obviously a wonderful friend."

Aster smiled. "I suspect her speech was to keep Mr. Bingley's eye and mind on her Jane, considering he was just complimenting Miss Lucas to Elizabeth."

A noise deep in his throat made it clear he disagreed with Mrs. Bennett's tactics. The next amusing noise from him was a soft snort when Mr. Bingley claimed he was pleased that Jane was at Netherfield being ill.

"Poor sap is clearly done for."

Giggling, Aster snuggled closer. A few scenes later, the cast was outside Netherfield, getting into the carriage. "Oh, this is my favorite part. Watch."

Thatch's attention was fixed to the screen.

After the hand flex moment, she gave a small squeal of delight.

"I don't get it," Thatch said.

"Back in that time, men and women didn't often

touch hands or skin. Women usually wore gloves. Dancing was one of the few times hand touching was appropriate, if gloves weren't worn. So that moment was a shock for Elizabeth, him taking her bare hand like that. And being in contact with her bare skin affected Mr. Darcy as well. The hand flex…he can still feel her hand…her skin, and I daresay he likes it."

Thatch nodded. "I get it now." His fingertips trailed up her arm. "For weeks, whenever I touched your skin, it was there on my skin like a memory."

She shivered. "And your touch was like a tattoo."

He continued to skim his fingers up and down her arm. "I like that."

During the ball at Netherfield, Aster enjoyed his insights.

"Turn around," he said when Elizabeth was looking for Mr. Wickham and Mr. Darcy appeared behind her.

The way Mr. Darcy looked at Elizabeth from behind before slipping out of the way always delighted Aster, but then Mr. Collins popped up.

"She doesn't want to lavish anything on you, you little creep of a man."

His statements became even more amusing during Elizabeth's dance with Mr. Dracy. After the second time they came face to face with the choreography, Thatch shook his head. "Two opportunities to kiss her wasted." The third time, with the discussion of Mr. Wickham heating the moment, he said, "If that were Paisley and Case, Case would've grabbed her right then and silenced her with a kiss."

"Because Case is clearly a gentleman."

Thatch chuckled. “Clearly.” He shifted to her. “Have you ever been to a ball like that?”

When would she have had the opportunity to go to a lavish ball? “Only in my dreams.”

He took her hand. “The Enchanted Hierarchy Ball is in a few weeks. Case has to go, as a faction leader. I’m going as his right-hand. Would you like to go?”

“Would I be allowed?”

“You’d be my date. Yes, you’d be allowed. And I’d like to see someone try to kick you out or bar you access. Not only would I rip them to pieces, but Case would tear apart whatever’s left.”

She couldn’t stop the smile. “I’m a lucky fairy having the two of you at my side, and, yes, I would love to go to the ball with you. As your date.”

Hand on her cheek, he kissed her until she sighed and cuddled into him again to watch Elizabeth and Mr. Darcy’s growing romance. The way Thatch paid attention to the movie was a constant entertainment. He physically cringed when Mr. Collins proposed to Elizabeth. “‘The violence of my affection’? Well, now, that is definitely Case.”

Aster supposed he was right. The way Case trashed this very parlor after Paisley left hinted at a violent affection, but he wouldn’t unleash that on Paisley. On furniture, sure. But on Paisley? Never.

Thatch’s growl drew her attention back to the TV. “The little bastard didn’t just say Elizabeth wouldn’t have another marriage proposal. What a little weasel. Someone needs to slap him around a bit.”

“I think her refusal slaps him around just fine.”

“Hm. Mary always seems to be looking at Mr.

Collins. I think she likes him."

"She certainly has sympathy for him. The two of them actually would've been a good pair. They seem to have the same ideals. But she was far too young for him."

A short time later: "Oh no, Charlotte, not Mr. Collins."

Aster laughed.

Her next favorite scene came. The one in the rain when Mr. Darcy admitted he loved Elizabeth. Aster bit her bottom lip, waiting for Thatch's reaction.

"Oh, damn, he's in love," Thatch said, and all Mr. Darcy had said was Elizabeth's name.

When Mr. Darcy pushed the three little words out as if speaking them was a struggle, so they had to be said almost as if they were one word, Thatch leaned back and stretched out his legs, which he crossed at the ankles, obviously pleased to have called it first.

"'Most ardently,'" he mumbled. "That's good."

When Elizabeth confronted Mr. Darcy with her accusations for ruining her sister's happiness, Thatch winced at Mr. Darcy's reaction. "Ouch."

Then the two characters were face to face again, heated in argument.

"Oh, just kiss her!"

"Kissing doesn't fix everything."

"But it can be a good start." He fell silent, though, when Elizabeth cut Mr. Darcy off at the knees.

The scene ended and Thatch remained silent until Mr. Darcy came to her after dark to bring her a letter. "She said he'd be the last person she'd be prevailed upon to marry, not that she'd *never* marry him. There's still hope."

Aster hugged his middle. "You're a hopeless romantic."

"Don't let that get around."

She laid her cheek against his chest. "It'll be our secret."

Through the rest of the movie, his comments remained entertaining. During the scene at sunrise in a fog-covered field, Thatch still couldn't believe they hadn't kissed when they had the perfect opportunity to do so.

"She kissed his hand," Aster pointed out. "That's a pretty powerful action."

The end credits went up, and the two of them stayed on the couch embracing.

"That's a great movie."

She smiled. "I'm glad you enjoyed it."

He shifted to kiss her temple. "I did. And I enjoyed watching it with you. So, who was the one who was proud and who was the one who was prejudice?"

"I daresay they were both extremely proud and very prejudiced."

"Hm." He grazed his fingers up and down her arm, lulling her to close her eyes. After a long moment of silence, he said something that had her opening her eyes. "Tomorrow, I'd like you to meet my grandparents.

14

Hedgehog

He didn't know what came over him in that moment, but he'd been wanting to bring Aster to meet his grandparents, to introduce them to the fairy he adored, for a long time. Now seemed like the perfect time.

Aster sat up and faced him. "Really? You do?"

He skimmed his thumb over her cheek. "I told you before, I want them to meet the fairy I'd die for."

She threw her arms around him in an embrace that tightened his chest. "I'd love to meet them. I truly would."

The tightening intensified, and he kissed the side of her neck. She was making him happier than he'd ever been. It almost wasn't fair considering she was waffling between the joy of being with him and sadness at being apart from Paisley. He could tell she was putting on a brave face for him, and he hated she felt she had to do that for him, but he hoped bringing her to meet his grandparents would lift her spirits. By the way she was smiling, it seemed to be doing the trick already.

The next day, though, she started to fret. She spent all morning in her bedroom, trying on one dress and then another and fussing over her hair. Thatch left her to do her thing, but when it was time for them to leave, he tapped gently on her door. "Aster, baby doll, we have to get going or we'll be late."

"Come in."

He eased the door open to find her standing in the middle of the floor that was littered

with her pretty dresses. She wore a pale yellow dress with a lavender flower print. Her violet hair was piled atop her head, speckled with real lavender blooms. A few strands of hair curled around the sides of her face. She looked absolutely beautiful, but a cloud of nerves danced around her as she twisted and turned to look at herself in the mirror.

"Do you think your grandma will like this dress?"

He blinked.

"And my hair. Should I put it down? Maybe the flowers are too much."

He approached. "What are you talking about, sweetheart?"

"I want to make a good impression."

He caught her shoulders when she started to twist around to look at herself from every angle again. "Baby doll, you look gorgeous. My grandparents aren't going to care about what you're wearing. You could wear a burlap sack, and you'd still make a good impression. You'd still be utterly beautiful. Whatever dress you wear, whether you have flowers in your hair or not, they will love you."

"Are you sure?"

He cupped her face with his hands, struck by her beauty and her nerves and that she could believe that anyone would think her anything but adorable. "I'm sure, sweetheart. It won't ever matter what you wear or do with your hair. You will charm them with your smile and laughter and every single word you say."

"Now I'm feeling overwhelmed."

He smiled. "Don't be. You have nothing to worry about." He leaned down to graze his lips over her forehead. "Trust me, okay?"

Her fingers curled into his shirt. "I just…I've never had a boyfriend whose grandparents I could meet. I don't know what I'm supposed to do."

"There's nothing you have to do. Be yourself. That's it."

She took a shaky breath. "Okay. I'm ready."

He kissed her forehead before taking her hand and walking her to the front door. Then he picked her up to cradle her in his arms and fly to the edge of the faye faction bordering the territory for the aelf faction. It was the safest place for his grandparents to hide out and live the rest of their lives, unthreatened by those who'd tear them apart, and not long ago…would've killed them. Even though it was the safest place for them, their home was still concealed. Only their family knew where to find it, hidden among oaks and ferns and vines with giant leaves.

Thatch landed on a small dirt path and set Aster on her feet. His grandparents' cottage was in front of them. Rows of colorful flowers circled the cottage.

"It's so pretty here."

"My grandparents spend all of their time in this garden, since they have nowhere else to go."

Aster stared up at him with wide eyes. "But surely they can live out in the open now, without fear of punishment. Case wouldn't allow anyone to harm your grandparents. And neither would Paisley."

"They only know what they'd lived. When they fell in love, it wasn't just forbidden for a demon and a fairy to marry and procreate. It was punishable by death. They don't trust the Enchanted Hierarchy to accept them. Or my dad. Or me."

She gripped his waist. "I won't let them hurt you."

The fierceness in her eyes and in her words made him smile. He bent down to kiss her gently on the lips. "That's supposed to be my line."

She shook her head. "I don't want you to get hurt, either, Thatch."

He kissed her again. "They're probably watching us from the window."

She giggled against his mouth.

Twining his fingers with hers, he led her to the door and knocked on the smooth wood. A moment later, it opened to his granddad, a demon with navy blue skin and horns a faded gray. He smiled at Thatch before turning his attention to Aster. And just like Thatch had done when he'd met Aster, his granddad dropped to one knee. Instead of placing a fist to the center of his chest, though, and vowing to protect her, he took Aster's hands in his and gazed up at her with awe in his eyes. "You are absolutely precious."

Thatch caught a glimpse of Aster's face. She was gaping at his granddad.

"Sweetheart, don't overwhelm her." A dainty hand whacked his granddad in the shoulder, and his grandma, with cherry blossom pink hair and wings like opal appeared at his side. "You have to forgive him, dear. He's a sucker for pretty fairies." She gave Aster a wide smile, which Aster returned. "We're thrilled you're here. Thatch has written to us about you, and we've been excitedly waiting for your visit."

Aster glanced at Thatch; he'd never told her he'd been writing to his grandparents about her.

"I'm Blossom," his grandma said, but Aster couldn't shake her hand because his granddad hadn't released hers yet. "Alright, Harland, let her hand go. You're starling her."

"I'm sorry, doll. Forgive me."

Doll? What were the odds of that?

Harland stood, but he was still holding Aster's hand. "Come inside. It's not every day I have two beautiful fairies under my roof."

Aster laughed and let Harland lead her into the house.

Thatch shut the door behind him.

"Come have a seat, Aster. I was making chamomile-lavender tea. It'll help to calm your nerves," Blossom said.

"Oh, that sounds lovely. I love lavender tea."

Harland brought Aster over to a couch and held out

a hand for her to sit. Then he nudged Thatch. "If you don't cuddle up next to her, I will."

"Harland!" Blossom laughed in the kitchen while prepping cups of tea. "Don't say that to him. Thatch, ignore him, dear. Your granddad has been giddy about you and Aster since your first letter."

Thatch lowered onto the couch next to Aster and put an arm around her.

She leaned into him.

Seeing that, Harland nodded in approval.

As Blossom came over with a tray full of tea, Harland intercepted her and took the tray from her hands.

"Harland, I can carry a tray of tea."

"Not when I'm here to carry it for you."

Thatch caught his grandma rolling her eyes behind his granddad's back, but she was smiling from ear to ear.

Harland bent forward to set the tray on the coffee table. "Don't think I didn't feel that eyeroll."

"I don't know what you mean." She sat on the identical couch across from them and patted the cushion beside her.

Harland took the spot next to her, lifted her hand to his lips, and kissed it. As Blossom blushed, Harland passed her a cup of tea.

Blossom took it and sipped the brew.

Thatch picked up a cup for Aster.

Their fingers brushed. The same spark of awareness he felt when their fingers grazed while passing Aster the cup of coffee the day they'd met happened again. He wondered if his grandparents still felt that when their hands touched. Needing to calm his own nerves, he picked up his cup and swallowed down the tea.

"Thatch, you're downing that tea like your life depends on it," Harland said as Thatch filled his cup to the brim again.

Aster rubbed his arm. Then she faced his grandparents. "If you don't mind, I'd love to know how the two of you met."

Harland grinned. "I used to patrol the borders of the daemon faction. This was back when stepping a foot or beating a wing inside another faction's territory was warrant for arrest or worse. I caught sight of a colorful flash of something and landed on the edge of our border to find a fairy with pink hair darting between trees. Curious, I followed, trying to figure out what a fairy was doing in our neck of the woods. For some reason, I was actually having fun sneaking behind the tiny fairy, who was scolding some critter that kept evading her. I'd never seen a creature so adorable in my life. I realized she was chasing after an injured hedgehog seconds before I noticed another demon zeroing in on her and *she* was about to be injured. Or worse. Fear like I'd never felt before pummeled me in the chest, and I tackled the other demon mere feet from her."

Blossom took Harland's hand and held it on her lap. "I was petrified. Seeing these two, big demons fighting just feet away from me, and not understanding that they were fighting *over* me until I heard Harland shout, 'She's just here for an injured hedgehog, you son-of-a-bitch!' I was positively shaking. Harland got the other demon to leave and then shocked the dandelion fluff out of me when he got down on his hands and knees and started to look for the hedgehog. After a moment, he peered up at me and said, 'Aren't you going to help?' He carried the hedgehog back for me, cuddling it against his wide chest, not caring about its sharp spines, and I was crushing on him by the time we reached the edge of the daemon faction."

"And it was love at first sight for me. It was a good thing I was already on my hands and knees when I asked her if she was going to help, because I would've fallen to my knees right then."

"It's quite a thing to see a demon on his knees, isn't it?" Blossom winked at Aster, who blushed up to her roots. "When we got to the faye faction, Harland told me that if I wanted to see him again, he'd like to know how the hedgehog was doing and to meet him back right at that same spot the next morning. Let's just say, I went, and I continued to go every day for weeks. Until we were discovered."

Aster squirmed. "What happened?"

"We were dragged away from each other by my fellow daemon guards," Harland said. "Hearing Blossom scream like that iced my blood."

Now, it was Thatch squirming. His arm flexed around Aster, tucking her even closer. He never wanted to know that feeling.

"He was beaten by his own people," Blossom said.

"But I escaped and went to the faye faction. They healed me. We wanted to stay there forever, but the daemon faction was hunting for me, and I knew they would come there. They'd target Blossom and torture every fairy until they found me. My parents came, the only ones who accepted my love for a fairy, and together with the faye faction, they got us out. This has been our home ever since." He lifted Blossom's hand and kissed her knuckles. "I've loved every second of it."

"Have you ever wanted to come back?" Aster asked.

Blossom shook her head. "What we did was illegal. While Case may not have us prosecuted, there are countless demons from that time who remember just how punishable that act was, and they remember *us*. They wouldn't stop trying to kill us, as they had wanted to do all those years ago."

Aster shivered, and Thatch stroked her arm.

Blossom studied their tea tray. "Oh, I forgot the cookies. Harland, will you lend me a hand?"

"Of course, my love."

Thatch leaned into Aster when his grandparents stepped into the kitchen. "You don't have to worry about anyone tearing us apart or coming after us. No one would have the gall to go against Case or me. Trust me, baby doll, we're safe."

"I know, but just thinking about how different it would've been if we'd been born a generation or two earlier, then we wouldn't be possible."

He disagreed. Their love would've been possible. It just wouldn't have been accepted. And he would've been as stubborn as his grandfather. He would've done anything to be with Aster then, just like he'd do anything now.

Harland set a plate of sugar cookies on the table. They had pretty flower-petal sprinkles on top.

Aster took one. When she bit into it, sugar clung to her lip, and a purple flower petal floated down from the cookie and landed on her lap.

Thatch plucked it off her skirt and set it on her plate.

"Do you want a bite?" she asked.

Such an innocent question, but it was a far from innocent answer that came to his lips when he whispered in her ear. "I want a bite out of you."

She cleared her throat. Her elbow tapped him in the ribs.

Smiling, he reached for his own cookie.

They engaged in small talk until it was time to begin dinner.

Aster stood at the same time as Blossom. "May I help? I love to cook."

"Of course. I'd love to have a fellow fairy in my kitchen."

As Aster and Blossom chopped vegetables and minced herbs in the kitchen, Thatch and Harland stayed in the living room to talk privately.

Harland leaned forward. "You wrote about a threat to her life. Are they still threatening her?"

Thatch glanced at Aster. "There hasn't been any more threats since Paisley left."

"Maybe it's a good thing Paisley left then."

Thatch would never blame Paisley for the threats against Aster. As it was, Aster would choose to have her best friend rather than be safe. She'd endure all the threats to have Paisley back again. "They might've set their sights on Aster to get to Paisley, but I don't believe she's safe until the bastards who threatened her life are out of the picture for good."

Harland nodded. "Agreed. They deserve all the pain for threatening someone so sweet and precious as your Aster."

Your Aster.

Aster was his.

And he was hers.

That thought never failed to tighten his stomach muscles. He gazed at her as she and his grandma laughed in the safety of a kitchen emitting delicious smells. Seeing his grandma safe and only wanting the same thing for Aster, he understood his granddad's decision to move out here and live their lives hidden away. Thatch would do the same for Aster.

Harland lowered his voice even more. "Have you told her yet that you love her?"

Thatch shifted on the small couch. "I think she knows." He hadn't exactly been shy about showing how he felt about her.

"Knowing and being told for certain are two different things. Have. You. Told. Her?"

Thatch shook his head. "Not yet."

"What are you waiting for?"

He shrugged, but he knew. He was waiting for Paisley to return. Only then would Aster truly be happy again and free to revel in his love.

"Don't wait long, Thatch. A creature as precious as that should know she's loved without a shadow of a doubt, and she should be shown that she's loved every moment of every day. Make sure you're the demon to do that."

A possessiveness had a growl rumbling in his

throat before he could stop it. “I’ll be the only one to love her. The. Only. One.”

Harland nodded. “That’s my boy.”

Aster joined him back on the couch a moment later. Her soft, warm body against his created a vise around his throat. Three words were stuck in there, tangling with his Adam’s apple. He swallowed them down. Not yet. Now wasn’t the time. But soon. Soon he’d tell her that she had his heart, and he wanted her to keep it forever.

Once dinner was ready, they sat at a small table really meant for two and ate a delicious vegetarian meal packed with fresh vegetables and herbs. Afterward, his grandparents stood with them on the doorstep, saying their goodbyes. Blossom and Aster hugged each other as Aster promised to visit soon.

“Visit anytime,” Harland said. “With or without Thatch.”

Aster smiled. “I will.”

“And you.” Harland pointed at Thatch. “Take care of her.”

Thatch swept her up in his arms. “Always.” Then he took off to bring her home.

15

Cinnamon

Aster was dizzy with need upon arrival at Case's mansion.

Wren met them at the door with a knowing smirk as Thatch set Aster on her feet and draped an arm around her shoulders to bring her to his side. "Hey, you two. You're pretty inseparable these days."

"I can't protect her if she's not near."

Aster frowned at Thatch's words. She'd thought he liked to be close for reasons other than protection. She'd thought he always had to be touching her, not because it'd be quicker to grab her in a moment of danger, but because touching her brought him pleasure.

Wren only smiled. "Case left for the Enchanted Hierarchy Council Meeting."

That meant the mansion was empty. Case wouldn't be back for another hour or so. Sometimes the meetings ran long. Considering he and Jude planned to tell the other faction leaders that Paisley had left, forfeiting her thrones, there was no telling how long this meeting would last. Aster would then be named the leader of the faye faction, and Silas would be the leader of the vampyre faction. Silas was ready, but Aster wasn't. She wasn't meant to be queen. Paisley was. But if tonight was going to be her last night before she was forced to take the throne to save the faye faction, she'd spend it getting Thatch to moan for her and say her name as he seethed in pleasure.

She took Thatch's hand. "Have a good night, Wren."

"You, too, Aster." The little spark in his dark blue eyes told her that he had an idea how Aster planned to have a good night. A very, very good night.

She led Thatch into the mansion and dragged him down the hall toward the library where she could be sure they'd have privacy if Case came home early. For this, she yearned to be anywhere but her bedroom, and she wanted to take charge, be a little reckless, a little adventurous, a little wild.

"Whoa, baby doll. What's your rush?"

She tugged him into the library and pushed him down onto a couch.

"Aster, what has—"

She lowered to her knees in front of him.

"—gotten into you?" He stared as his body became rigid.

She laid her hands on his knees.

His eyes dilated.

She slid her hands up his thighs.

His chest strained against his shirt when he inhaled.

She drew down the zipper of his pants.

His hands became fists.

She coaxed out his cock. It was hard and thick and hot in her hand.

"Baby doll—"

Eyes on his, she leaned forward and slicked her tongue up the length of him to the sleek head of his cock.

He knocked his head back. "Diablo."

Enjoying his reaction, she swirled her tongue just around the tip, reveling in the silkiness of his shaft's head against her tongue. His cock was so beautiful—violet like the rest of him and smooth like marble. She wanted to tell him this, but she had her mouth full when she fused her mouth around the tip and sucked. At the same time, she gently squeezed his dick with both of her hands stacked on top of each other.

"Oh fuck."

Thatch had never said the f-word around her before. With the way Case talked, she was pretty sure he'd never said the f-word once in his life. The fact she was the one who pried the word out of him gave her a surge of power.

At the base of his cock, she continued to palpitate her hand, squeezing and then releasing him. On and on.

With her other hand, she pumped her fist up and down his impressive length. So good. So damn good. The texture of his hot, tight skin made her mouth water. He tasted like sea salt and…how could he taste like cinnamon? She didn't care as she sucked harder. All that mattered was that she got her fill of him and his taste.

"Aster, oh, fuck. Aster, baby, that feels so good." His fingertips grazed her cheek and circled around her ear as he tucked the hair that framed her face back from her cheek.

She looked up at him again.

"Diablo, you're so beautiful."

Her lips twitched around his girth in a smile, but she didn't stop.

She flicked her tongue along the slit in the tip of his cock, collecting the drops of pre-cum. There was the odd cinnamon flavor again, with a hint of musk. He groaned as she licked it up, and she moaned, because he really was delicious.

While exploring his cock, she accidentally located a little strip on the underside of his head that made him seethe. She stroked that spot with the tip of her tongue and was rewarded with seeing him unravel. He gripped the edge of the couch. His hips contracted and lifted off the cushion. His chest rose and fell rapidly, threatening to pop every button on his shirt. The veins in his neck pulsated. His eyelids fluttered. A bead of sweat trailed down his throat.

Turned on by his reaction, she clenched her thighs together and wrapped her lips around him again. She couldn't take him very far, but she was able to twirl her tongue around him.

Suddenly, one of his hands lifted from the grip on the cushion. His fingers dove into her hair, poking holes into her updo. He didn't push her head down, just held on as if for dear life.

"I'm going to come, baby."

Those five words sent a surge of lust and excitement through her. She switched from licking to sucking, and that single act sealed it. He growled as he came, filling her mouth. She swallowed down his cum and continued to slurp on his cock until it stopped bucking in her hands and it'd pumped the last of him over her tastebuds.

When she shifted back, he was panting and quivering, and it was the sexiest thing she'd ever seen—a demon trembling after getting his cock sucked and drained.

Still kneeling between his legs, she smiled. "You cursed."

He opened his eyes and focused on her. After a moment, he took a deep breath. "I did." He pushed to his feet. Her face was in front of his crotch as he rezipped his pants, and she could do nothing but kneel there and stare. Then he hauled her to her feet and set her on the couch.

The cushion was warm from his body heat, and she melted into it.

He lowered to his knees and began parting her thighs. Inch by inch. The entire time he widened her legs, he held eye contact. He continued to hold eye contact while peeling her panties down her legs to her ankles and off her feet. The only time he looked away was when he settled his face between her shaking thighs and licked his tongue right up her pussy.

She knew she was soaking wet, and she was aware that he was licking up all her arousal.

That turned her on even more. The attention he gave her pussy, following her contours, swirling around her opening, tickling her clit, lavishing every millimeter, had her writhing and whimpering and waiting for the moment he'd let her come, but he ate her so slowly, so thoroughly that all she could do was clutch his arms and sink deeper into the sensations he created.

"Thatch. Thatch, please. Please."

In answer, he formed his lips around her clit and began to suck it.

"Yes, oh, yes." She ground against his mouth, encouraging pressure in one millisecond and withdrawing from it the next. Over and over.

Her chanting had him eating her with a hunger that stunned her.

She cried out. And cried out. And cried out.

Finally, her orgasm came. It slammed into her with such force that her vision went dark. So strong it was that she couldn't even hear herself, but the way her throat felt strained told her she'd no doubt screamed.

Thatch continued to lick her pussy even after she came, cleaning up the fresh cum that dripped from her. She started to squirm, moan, tremor. Her second orgasm stole her breath.

Now, Thatch kissed her cunt, placing little pecks up the length of her, from opening to clit. He finished with kisses along the inside of her thighs before picking up her boneless body and placing her on his lap. She was so sated and stunned that she lay heavily against his chest. Thatch didn't seem to mind one bit. He caressed her back and whispered the sweetest of sweet nothings into her ear.

After some time, she slid off his lap and onto the cushion beside him.

He angled toward her to play with one of the loose strands of her hair. "That was surprising, baby doll."

"Surprising good?"

He grinned. "Very good."

The front door slamming made her flinch.

"Case is home."

Silence followed.

"Should we check on him?" she asked.

"No. However that meeting went, he'll want to be alone right now."

"Right."

She laid her head on his shoulder and draped her arm across his abdomen to hold onto him. Being quiet with Thatch, cuddling on a couch or love seat or in bed, was one of her favorite things to do. Silent snuggles was one of her love languages, as it turned out, and she hoped they spoke it every day at least once.

A second door slam.

Aster jerked again.

Case must be in a really bad mood.

She hated that Case was in so much pain, ravaged by rage and grief.

If only Paisley would write to him, call him, come back to him…

Aster turned her head to the library's entrance right as Case stepped inside, carrying Paisley in his arms.

16

Gold Masks & Purple Dildos

Seeing Aster and Paisley hug filled Thatch with relief. Finally, things would get back to normal. That same relief pulsed off Case, but his shoulders were still tensed.

Case stepped closer to the embracing best friends. "Paisley needs some of your healing magick, cutie pie."

When Aster shifted back, Paisley held out her hands.

Aster's gasp had Thatch inching forward to get a look—burns. All over Paisley's wrists.

"How'd this happen?" Aster asked, her voice horror-stricken.

"Iron restraints."

And that explained Case's tension.

"But how?" Aster asked.

"I was kidnapped."

Thatch's gaze snapped to Case. *Kidnapped*?

Case gave a stiff nod.

"That's why I've been gone," Paisley continued. "I didn't leave. I certainly wouldn't have left and not told you where I was going."

Thatch joined Aster's side. "Who did this?"

"I don't know. They wore gold masks. I think they had wings, though."

He tilted his head. "How do you know?"

"It's a hunch, but to bring me where they held me undetected, they likely flew. I was all the way in the mountains, close to Fier Mountain."

Fier Mountain could only mean one thing…

"Enya," Case growled.

Exactly Thatch's thought. Enya, the fier faction's queen.

Paisley shook her head. "I don't think so, though. When I escaped, I stumbled out into the sun, and they didn't follow. They easily could've gotten me back. I couldn't move fast, and two of them could've hunted me down. They either didn't have their masks or…they are vampires."

Vampires? Paisley's own faction. No, they wouldn't dare. Would they?

Case's jaw worked. "If they were vampires, then there's a chance they could've known about the underground tunnel."

Aster bent her neck.

That damned tunnel.

Thatch reached out a hand to Aster and curled a comforting hand around her shoulder. She met his eye, and he gave her a gentle squeeze. While Paisley and Case discussed the tunnel, Thatch did his best to silently assure her that everything would be okay. He needed her to believe this wasn't her fault, now that someone could've used that tunnel to kidnap Paisley.

"Cutie pie, we still need that healing."

Case's voice had Aster jumping. "Oh, sorry." She scrambled to heal Paisley's burns, but just because they were gone didn't mean everything was right.

Nothing was right.

A queen had been kidnapped and tortured.

Nothing would be right until they paid back the bastards who'd caused all this.

Case carried Paisley off to further tend to her, and Thatch called Silas and Jude, instructing them to get to Case's immediately. They had business to conduct that required all the people who cared about Paisley. It didn't take long for either of them to arrive.

Shortly after, Paisley and Case came downstairs, both of them dressed for a nighttime mission. Even Aster had changed into all black—a tight shirt that hugged her breasts and leggings that showed off that lovely butt of hers in all its shapely glory. She'd even twined her hair into a bun. Clearly, she thought she was joining them on this mission to hunt down the gold masks in the cave where they'd held Paisley against her will, but he couldn't allow Aster to come.

"Someone kidnapped the vampyre queen," Silas said. "They will pay for this."

Case nodded. "They will pay with their lives."

"Yes, they will."

Thatch couldn't agree more. "Let's go." Except one of them would be staying behind. He faced Aster. "Baby doll—"

She crossed her arms. "Don't you dare try to tell me I'm staying here." Her lavender gaze pinned him like a dart to a target. "I'm going with you."

Countless words of refusal were on the tip of Thatch's tongue.

Aster grabbed his hand and squeezed to show him how insistent she was, but her eyes already did that. "She's my family. She's the *only* family I have left. Just as much as Case and Silas want revenge, I do, too. I'm going."

His jaw flexed as he pondered what he could say, if anything, to convince her to stay here, out of harm's way. Would asking her to stay *for him* work? Because if anything happened to her, the pain would be excruciating.

"Thatch, she's coming," Case said, going against every single one of Thatch's protector instincts. "And you'll make sure nothing happens to her."

But that right there. That spoke to his fierce need to keep Aster safe. "That doesn't even need to be said." If she had to be in the thick of things, then he'd be her shield.

Paisley and Case walked to a patch of woods at the edge of Case's property. She'd decided to fly, and they were all respecting her wishes to stay back so she could summon her wings away from their prying eyes. Just the fact she wanted to fly among them, though, even shrouded in darkness, was a big deal.

Thatch turned Aster to face him. He ran his hands down her arms. “I’ve never seen you in all black.” He lowered his voice. “Or in something so form-fitting.” He cupped her hips before gliding his hands around to her butt. “I like it.”

“You do, do you?” She shivered as his hands slipped up her back.

“Mm-hm.” He curved his hands to the sides of her breasts. “Oh, yeah, I do.” And because he couldn’t resist how amazing her breasts felt encased by the tight top, he grazed his thumbs over them.

She bit her bottom lip. “Thatch. We’re about to go on a life-or-death mission here. Stop feeling me up,” she hissed.

He crushed his mouth to hers. “Don’t call it life-or-death,” he said against her lips. “The only ones dying tonight are the bastards who hurt Paisley.”

“Well, of course they are, dummy.”

The sounds of two sets of wings beating against the air drew their attention.

“Now let’s go help our besties get their vengeance.”

Smirking, he lifted her into his arms, relishing how good her curves felt in that skin-tight little number against his palms. He took off, followed by Silas. Below them, Jude galloped with fury. Every single one of them wanted payback, and they all intended to get it.

The journey was a long one. What helped to pass the time was Aster’s kisses on his neck and her sweet question every so often if he was tired of carrying her. No, he wasn't tired of carrying her. Even if his arms did start to strain, he'd simply heft her onto his shoulder and keep on going. It wasn't logical, considering she could fly, but love wasn't always logical, and he *had* to hold her. There was no way around it. He loved holding her, having her close, pressed to his chest. Those kisses, though, were making it hard for him to stay focused on the task at hand.

Her sweet lips fluttered over his neck again, and his cock responded to that. His grip on her tightened, and he clenched his jaw. "Baby doll, you're going to have to stop that."

"I'm sorry. Your neck is prime kissing real estate, and it's right in front of my face. If you don't like it, though, then I'll—"

"If I don't like it? Baby doll, I'm hard. I like it plenty. I would just rather not be hard right now."

"Oh, right." She dropped her gaze. "I wasn't thinking. I'm sorry."

He shook his head. "Stop apologizing, sweetheart. I love your kisses. I *want* your kisses. When this is over, you can kiss me all you want. And I'll kiss you all I want, too."

She nuzzled his neck. "Is this okay?"

He swallowed. "Perfect."

When Paisley and Case touched down, Thatch landed, too, and set Aster on her feet. They continued on foot, and he clasped Aster's hand the entire way. None of them said a word, couldn't risk it. Instead, Thatch and Aster communicated with touch. Thatch swept his thumb over the back of her hand, and she clung to his arm, stroking his bicep absently. He had a feeling that touching him like that soothed her. Diablo, she shouldn't be here. She should be safe in Case's mansion with the ring of demons posted around the property and Wren keeping an eye on her. Not out here in the middle of the nowhere, on the same path Paisley had taken when she'd fled from her captors. If someone could've done that to the vampyre and faye queen, there was no telling what they'd do to sweet little Aster.

He'd rip anyone to shreds if they so much as tried to harm his fairy.

Break them into pieces.

Rip their skin from their bodies.

Scatter their bones.

Nothing would be left of them.

Paisley stopped at the edge of the woods. Up ahead was the cave where she'd suffered things he wasn't sure he'd ever know about, as it wasn't for him to know. If she told Case, that was between them. But it didn't matter what'd happened. They'd held her there against her will. Hurt her. Tortured her. He didn't need to know the details. The bastards would pay all the same.

At the cave entrance, they paused while Paisley used her vampire vision to peer into the darkness. Thatch wondered at how Case could contain himself. If Thatch were him, he'd be plopping Paisley off to the side and rushing in with the intent to kill. Case stuck beside Paisley every step of the way into that cave, though. Thatch followed them, holding onto Aster's hand, prepared to protect her at all costs. Her *and* Paisley. Not a single one of them, Aster included, would let Paisley come to harm in those caves again.

Thatch could make out Paisley and Case in front of them but nothing beyond. The cave was pitch black and silent. He couldn't even make out the sound of dripping water. Nothing to indicate even a bat lived in the cave.

Suddenly, Paisley and Case halted.

Thatch tugged Aster to a stop and yanked her to his side.

"They're ahead," Paisley whispered. "I can hear them. They're…the fuckers are playing poker."

For them to be acting like nothing had happened, it enraged Thatch. "What's our gameplan?" *And please let it involve a lot of blood.*

While Silas and Jude offered ideas on how they thought the bastards should be punished, Thatch held Aster firmly to his side. Should they torture them into confession in Case's dungeons as Silas wanted or slaughter them and dump them at their factions as Jude wanted? Thatch wasn't sure which option was best. Just as long as they suffered in some way.

Case turned toward where Paisley had stood. "What do you think? Pais?"

Thatch's spine snapped straight.

Paisley was gone.

Crashing sounds carried from deeper in the cave.

"Fuck." Case took off.

Thatch deposited Aster behind him. "Stay back." And he took off after Case.

Inside a chamber carved into the cave, Paisley was on top of a figure wearing a gold mask. She'd ripped out their throat, coating herself in their blood. Beside her, a small foldable table had been knocked over, sending their poker chips and cards across the ground.

Case hadn't hesitated but sprang right into the mix to fight alongside Paisley. He wrenched one of their necks, snapping their spine.

Thatch, Silas, and Jude launched into the chamber to defend Paisley and Case. While Thatch caught one of them by the back of his shirt and flung him into a wall, Jude kicked another one, giving Silas the opportunity to jump on him.

Thatch was moving in on the gold mask he'd stopped from escaping when Paisley cut him off. The scream that left her made his blood cold, and he watched her sink her fist into the gold mask with a sickening sound.

The suspect crumpled, joining his three dead comrades.

Case hurried to Paisley and lifted his shirt to swipe the blood that drenched her chin. "What the hell, Paisley?"

A movement out of the corner of Thatch's eye had him turning to see Aster in the entrance to the chamber. Her wings were stiff on her back as she took in the carnage. He held up a hand to indicate for her to stay there and squatted down to remove the mask from one of the suspects' faces.

"We should've questioned them first," Case told Paisley.

Thatch shook his head. "I don't think there's any need for that." He parted the bastard's lips to reveal the sharp fangs.

"He was a vampire," Aster whispered.

They all had been. Members of Paisley's own faction had kidnapped her, tortured her, threatened her into giving up her thrones. Her *own* faction. This couldn't stand.

Except Paisley didn't want anyone to know what they'd done. If they did, others could get it into their heads that they could attempt the same. Instead, she decided to incinerate the evidence that any of this had happened by burning their bodies with dragon's fire, so Paisley and Case went off alone to Fier Mountain to seek Phoenix's assistance. Phoenix, a close friend to Paisley and the heir to the fier faction, was the only dragon shifter that could be trusted.

A dragon shifter returned with them and set the vampires aflame.

Paisley and Case took off as the bodies burned. Thatch didn't want Aster to have to stand there and watch the vampires turn to ash, so Thatch swept her up into his arms and took off.

The threat to Paisley was gone. The vampires who'd harmed her were burning away to nothing. Paisley would be safe now. And Aster, too. She wouldn't need him anymore. The thought of that had him clutching her tighter. She didn't kiss his neck, though, as he now hoped she would. The trip back to Case's was faster than the one to the cave, and he was reluctant to let her go, but he set her down so they could walk through the door.

Case did the opposite and picked Paisley up. "We're showering together," he said to Paisley, although he wasn't quiet about it. "And then I'm going to fuck you to sleep." Far from quiet. Case shot Thatch a look from over his shoulder. "Feel free to celebrate with Aster in a similar fashion."

Paisley whacked Case in the shoulder. "Don't say that to them."

"Baby, they deserve it. Just like we do." And he carted Paisley upstairs to live up to his promise.

Thatch glanced down at Aster. The idea of putting Aster to sleep from an orgasm he'd given her filled Thatch with so many ideas of what he could do to accomplish that.

She bit her bottom lip.

"Don't pay attention to him, baby doll."

"What if…what if I want to celebrate like that with you?"

Thatch sucked in a breath. "Baby…"

"I want you to feel me up, Thatch. I want you to peel off these leggings. I want you to fuck me to sleep."

Thatch gaped as blood rushed to his cock. "I'm not going to survive you, am I?"

She flattened her hands to his stomach, making the muscles there tighten with lust. "Oh, I'll be gentle on you. I promise."

Her words stunned him. "Baby doll, I can give you orgasms in a hundred different ways. With my fingers. My tongue. My lips. My dick stroking your pretty vulva, but I told you…you're too small, too tight. I'd tear you. Hurt you. I can't do that."

She broke eye contact. "Okay."

Diablo, he didn't want to upset her or make her feel as though he didn't want her in all the ways. He did. Diablo, did he want her. But he just couldn't hurt her. She was too precious, too delicate. He stroked her jaw. "Baby doll, are you mad at me?"

She shook her head. "No." Her pretty lavender

eyes met his. "Could you try something with me…for me?"

He grazed her jaw with his thumb. "Anything."

The next thing he knew, he stood in her bedroom, holding a purple dildo. He gaped at it. "How long have you had this?"

Her cheeks flared pink. "A…a while. I've never used it before, so I thought…maybe *you* could use it…on me."

All the rest of his blood flooded to his cock. "Yeah, baby, I'll use this on you. Climb onto your bed."

When she scrambled onto her bed, her wings fluttered rapidly.

He chuckled. "Sweetheart, any more excited and you'd be floating up to the ceiling."

"Any more excited and I'd be slipping right off this mattress."

He blinked. "Diablo."

She nodded. "Show me what you can do with that dildo."

He clenched his jaw and approached the bed. "Did you get a purple dildo for a reason, baby doll?"

She bit her bottom lip, and her gaze settled on his erection.

In his hand, the dildo was slimmer than his cock, but the color was spot on. He could slip it into her pretty pussy and not have to worry about hurting her, and he could imagine it was his own cock stroking inside her. Diablo, he wanted her to come all over that dildo.

He set the dildo beside her and knelt on the bed.

She quivered as he caressed her body through the

tight clothes encasing her curves. Her nipples poked at her top, and he swirled the tip of his finger over her right nipple. She moaned and arched her back. The action had her breasts pushing against his hand. He answered that plea by palming her breasts. Diablo, the feel of her round, heavy breasts in the silky material stretched over them was enough to have his cock twitching. He pinched her nipples, and her hips lifted.

When he removed her top, her wings slipped through the slits in the back of the fabric almost like water before springing back into shape. Her violet hair cascaded over her pillows, and his gaze feasted on her amazing breasts. Unable to resist, he bent down to swirl the tip of his tongue around her silky areolas before taking her breasts into his mouth one at a time. He only stopped sucking on them at the sound of her first whimpers.

She pouted at him, clearly craving more, and he brought his hands to her hips. That pout transformed into a gasp. She lifted her hips so he could peel those tight leggings off her legs. Underneath, she was bare. His mouth watered. He pushed her legs apart and settled between her lush thighs. And even though she needed to be wet for the dildo, he couldn't stop himself from dipping down and licking up her juices. "Diablo, you taste so good." He said that with his lips still against her vulva.

She shuddered.

As he licked her, he reached for the dildo. He glanced up to see her eyes were closed. She was fully engrossed in what he was doing that she wasn't aware he had the dildo now. Keeping his tongue on her clit, he pressed the button on the dildo's shaft. Not even the sound of its buzzing penetrated her pleasure. Only when he pressed the head to her opening did she jolt and make an adorable squealing noise.

He grinned. "How does that feel, baby?"

"Oh, Goddess."

He glided the tip through her slick lips.

Her body rolled like an ocean wave. "Goddess, that's amazing."

He tilted his head. "You haven't played with it yourself?"

"No. I…got it…for you."

He circled the tip over her clit. "For me?"

She moaned. "Y-yes. So you could do this."

"This right here? Tease your swollen clit?"

"Mm-hm."

"And this?" He glided the dildo up and down, parting her labia with the head already sleek with her arousal.

"Oh."

He took that as a yes. "And this?" He slid the dildo's tip into her.

She gasped. Her eyelids flipped open.

Staring into her eyes, he continued to slip the dildo inside her until it was in up to his fingers. "And this?" He worked the dildo slowly in and out, relishing that he was able to sink deeper inside her than his fingers could reach, and wishing that it were his cock and not something made of silicone.

"Oh, yes, yes."

He angled the dildo to hit her g-zone.

Her eyes rolled back.

Tickling her g-zone with the vibrator, seeing her face and chest flush and hearing her sexy and sweet noises as she came undone, unraveled him. Kneeling between her legs, he unzipped his pants with his free hand. His erection was there and ready when his hand fisted around it. He matched the pace of his left hand on his cock to his right hand on the dildo. Doing this, he could almost pretend that he was the one inside her, and it was her internal muscles clenching him and not his own hand.

Watching her face, listening to her moans, it became the truth.

She wailed, and he gripped his dick so hard that he came with her. His cum splashed between her thighs and onto the dildo.

A feral need overtook him, and he continued to work the dildo in and out of her so that his cum could mix with hers and seep inside her. If only he could fill her for real. He was so relentless in his desire that she was shattering again with another orgasm.

He eased the dildo out of her as her legs shook, tucked away his dick, and even though he needed to clean his cum off her, he gathered her close. Holding her as she lay there, stunned, was the highlight of his night. It didn't take her long before she fell asleep.

After a while, he shifted her onto the bed. She didn't so much as stir in her sleep. The fact he'd clearly knocked her out brought a smile to his face. He stepped into the bathroom, wet a hand towel with warm water, and brought it into the bedroom. Seeing her lying there, naked and content, tightened his chest with a dozen needs. He gently opened her legs again and laid the folded, warm towel over her vulva.

She let out a cute sigh, but she didn't wake. How she felt safe with him enough to let him clean her up, and she didn't so much as crack an eyelid open, meant so much to him. Once she was clean, he gathered her up in his arms again.

Embracing her, he whispered in her ear, "I love you, Aster."

The next day, he and Aster were walking hand-in-hand on Case's vast lawn when Paisley and Case found them. They were also holding hands, but Thatch was wise enough not to point it out. Those two were complicated. They worked well together but butted heads constantly, and yet, they were perfect.

Even though Thatch had quickly looked away from their joined hands, Paisley suddenly looked embarrassed and pried her hand from Case's. She didn't notice the way Case looked at her, as though she'd chopped off his hand at the wrist, but Thatch had.

"I'd like to spend some time with my best friend," Paisley said to Thatch, "if you don't mind."

How could he deny that? "Of course not." He lifted Aster's hand to his lips and kissed it. Then he backed away to let Paisley and Aster stroll ahead.

Case stepped up beside him.

Thatch stuffed his hands into his pockets. "Shouldn't we follow them?"

"The threat has been eliminated. I think they can walk alone." Still, Case took a step in their direction.

Thatch took one, too. "They can definitely walk alone."

"Don't need us to tail them." Case continued to follow.

"Nope. Don't need us."

"But maybe we could trail behind. To be sure."

"Yeah." Now they were moving at a slow, steady pace. "Just to be safe."

They fell into silence as they did just that.

Paisley suddenly halted, jolted toward Aster, and then darted a quick look over her shoulder at Case.

That from Paisley was odd.

The two of them stopped.

Up ahead, Paisley said something to Aster that they couldn't hear, and Aster responded.

Curiosity filled Thatch. What were they saying to each other?

Paisley whipped back to the front. Far from Paisley behavior.

A moment later, the two women started to walk again.

Thatch and Case followed suit. "What in the world do you think that was about?" Thatch asked.

Case jutted a shoulder. "How the hell am I supposed to know? I'm far from a Paisley whisperer, but…" He jabbed an elbow at Thatch. "I hear you're a fairy whisperer. The faye faction loves you."

Thatch shrugged as embarrassment settled on his shoulders. "I've just helped them when they needed it."

"You're a really good demon, Thatch. Too damn

good to be a demon in my opinion."

The truth was on the tip of Thatch's tongue. He wanted to tell Case that he didn't only have demon blood in his veins but fairy blood, too. All the years they'd known each other, he hadn't found the right time to tell his best friend the secret his family had kept hidden for so long. He opened his mouth to tell Case now, but the words froze in his throat when Aster tripped on her adorable bare feet. Instead of righting herself and continuing on, she glanced over her shoulder at him with the widest eyes he'd ever seen.

He jolted at the shock on her face. "What the hell?" he whispered.

At the same time, Case muttered, "What the fuck?"

Paisley's laughter carried over to them. She put an arm around Aster and coaxed her back around.

"Okay, seriously, what the hell are they talking about?" Thatch demanded.

"You're asking me as though I know the ways of women."

"You've known more women than most."

Case chuckled softly. "Paisley and Aster are another ballpark, my friend. What they discuss is not for us to know."

Thatch nodded. Women, and best friends at that, shared things with each other that no one outside of that had any right in knowing. It was precious. Nothing like the friendship between men. And far from that of demons.

Paisley and Aster went to the small garden on the side of Case's property where Aster had planted asters, violets, rosemary, and lavender. They were admiring the flowers and herbs while the two demons admired *them*. Neither demon said a word; lost in their own thoughts about the women kneeling there in the dirt. They looked so beautiful there in the sunlight that Thatch was speechless.

The moment vanished when Paisley shot a deadly glare over her shoulder right at Thatch. Her eyes were glowing red. He'd never seen that before. The sight was amazing and terrifying at once. The realization that vampire rage was aimed at him had him backing away.

Case did the same.

Paisley said something while still glaring at him.

Aster replied.

After a moment, her eyes faded back to normal.

Danger averted, but what the hell would've caused that reaction? Him? What the hell did he do?

The two women whispered to each other.

Aster gave him a shy look with flushed cheeks that intrigued him. She turned away, and Case arched a brow at Thatch.

"That look said so much."

"What exactly did it say?" Thatch asked.

"Passion, Thatch. It spoke volumes of passion."

He inhaled. "And the look Paisley gave me?"

"Oh, that? She wanted to kill you."

He shifted to Case. "For what?"

"Considering you're in love with her bestie, take a guess."

He swallowed. "That obvious?"

Case smiled. "Oh yeah."

Aster let out a happy squeal and embraced Paisley. That squeal was apparently because she and Paisley were going to have a slumber party watching movies and doing pedicures and eating popcorn. Aster looked up at him with smiling eyes. “Is that okay?”

He frowned and twirled a lock of her hair. “Why are you asking me that?”

“Because…well, we’ve been sleeping together at night.”

He smiled. “I’ll eventually fall asleep alone. Have fun with Paisley.”

“Thank you!” She pecked a quick kiss to his lips and skipped away.

He and Case watched a *Rocky* marathon while the girls had their fun. After the fourth movie, they went their own way. Thatch went to his room, showered, and stretched out in bed. Funny how quickly he’d gotten used to sleeping with Aster beside him or in his arms or snuggled against his chest. It took him hours to finally drift off. Soon after he did, his mattress shifted beneath him and a tiny, warm body slipped into place to be the small spoon to his big spoon. He hooked his arm around her and tucked her even closer. “What are you doing here, baby doll?”

“Paisley left. I woke up and missed you.”

He kissed her temple. “It’s crazy, but I missed you, too.”

“Well, I’m here now.”

He tightened his hold on her. “Yes, you are.”

Except, when he opened his eyes a few hours later, he was alone.

17

Completely, Perfectly, and Incandescently Happy

Aster loved to see the sunrise. The start of a new day was wonderous to behold. The fantastic colors streaking across the sky. The dew still clinging to flowers. The slight chill in the air because the sun hadn't yet set her warmth upon the land. Every part of it was magickal, and she liked to witness them as much as possible. Since the threats began, she hadn't been able to indulge in a single sunrise. Now that the threat had been eliminated, she wanted to bask in the yellows and oranges and purples, and even the pinks of a day promising a storm.

She strolled through the field beside Case's mansion. Wildflowers of all different species grew together in tangles of tall grass. She skimmed her hands over the blooms, feeling the wetness of dew that clung to her palms. The air was scented with the damp petals and earth. Beneath her bare feet, the grass was soft, muffling her steps. Still, even when she couldn't hear his footfall, she sensed him approaching and turned to see Thatch walking toward her like Mr. Darcy moving with purpose toward Elizabeth in that field after his aunt had visited. Except Thatch was shirtless and so handsome that it rooted Aster to the spot.

Thatch stopped before her. His hand cradled the side of her face. "You shouldn't be out here alone."

She laid her hand against his. "But I'm not alone."

"I didn't like waking up and not having you."

She smiled. "I might not have been in your bed, but you will always have me."

His chest rose and fell slowly. Then he bent over and pressed his lips to hers. As she kissed him back, he hauled her onto tiptoe so her body was flush against his. The passion of his kiss made her lightheaded and wet, and it sent her heart into excited, fluttering beats. She clung to him as he both weakened her and exhilarated her. His tongue glided against hers, drawing out moans. His lips sucked hers, making her sigh. And when his fingers crawled beneath her nightgown and tickled her clit, she whimpered. She wanted more.

Needed more.

She eased their lips apart. “Thatch, do you trust me?”

“That’s an odd thing to ask while I stroke your pussy, baby.”

She shivered. That was the first time he’d said the word ‘pussy’ aloud, and it excited her. “I have to know if you trust me.”

He rubbed her clit, and she let out a moan. “Yes, baby doll. I trust you.”

“G-good.” She grasped his arms as he continued to send her clit into ecstasy. “Th-there’s something I learned. My fairy dust can help us.”

He titled his head. At the same time, he shifted his fingers to brush her clit at a different angle. She cried out from the touch. “What do you mean?” he asked.

“I…” It was hard to think while his fingers drove her toward climax. “A little of my fairy dust on your…” Shimmers in her clitoris gland had her eyes rolling back. “…cock and between my…” Her thighs began to tremble. “legs would…would…” She moaned. “…allow us to…” She was panting now. “…have…” She was so close. “…sex.” And right when she felt she could’ve wailed her release, Thatch’s clever fingers ceased their movement and her orgasm faded.

“What?”

She blinked her eyelids open. “Th-that’s what Paisley told me yesterday.”

His brows furrowed. “The two of you discussed us having sex?”

The thought he could be mad at her for sharing something so intimate with someone beyond the two of them filled her with searing shame. “Well…sort of. She’s my best friend, and she said—”

He cradled the side of her face with his palm. “Your fairy dust can really make it so I won’t hurt you?”

She frowned. “Did you never wonder how your grandparents procreated?”

His gaze flicked to the side. “I…you can’t just ask your grandparents how they manage to have sex. Maybe my grandfather isn’t as b—” He shook his head as if to banish that thought. “Or maybe they’ve never had sex and used other methods for her to get pregnant like—”

She laid her hand against his to calm him. “Apparently our dust is how fairies can have sex with all different creatures. Orcs…centaurs…” She batted her lashes. “Demons…”

His thumb caressed her jawline. “I won’t hurt you?”

She shook her head. “No, and it only needs to be done once.”

Still, he appeared hesitant.

“I need you to trust me now, Thatch. Trust me and my fairy dust.”

Then she stepped away from him so that his hand appeared out from under her skirt. Smiling at him, she untied her satchel of fairy dust that always dangled at her hips. She took his same hand with fingers still coated with her arousal and laid the satchel in the center of his palm. As he stared at it in wonder, she slipped her nightgown off. When it tumbled down her legs to puddle around her ankles, his gaze snapped up to her naked body. His eyes widened. His pupils dilated. His chest expanded.

He stayed right there, watching her pick up her nightgown, spread it out on the ground, and lay on top of it. His gaze roved over her, lingering on her breasts before pausing at the apex of her thighs. And while his attention was affixed there, she opened her legs so he could see her swollen clit that he'd been teasing and her glistening labia, spread for him to reveal her pink opening, ready for him.

His lips parted as he sucked in a breath.

"Come here, Thatch."

His entire body trembled. "If I could dive into you, I would." A second later, he dropped to his knees and was plunging toward her as if he were really going to attempt diving into her, but his hands, on either side of her, held him up, and he sank down to kiss her so thoroughly that it felt like diving into a bottomless ocean. He worked his way down her neck and across her collarbones. When she expected him to lavish kisses over her breasts, he pushed up to admire them instead and said, "Diablo, your breasts are amazing."

A groan left him as he bent back down. What she yearned for she got when he opened his mouth and took her left breast into his hot cavern. He sucked on the soft mound, and she moaned. Her breast had started to tingle right at the moment he shifted to her right breast and fused his mouth to it.

She dug her fingertips into his sides. More heat and more of that slippery wetness pooled between her legs. She tightened her thighs around him.

He understood her quiet request and continued his journey down her chest and stomach to her pussy where he feasted on all the wet heat that had collected there.

She grasped his horns.

Her thighs quivered.

Her eyelashes fluttered.

But, no, she didn't want to orgasm yet.

Not yet.

She needed him inside her in a way he had never been inside her.

Stretching.

Filling.

Deeply stroking.

"Thatch. Thatch, please, I want your cock. Please."

He wheeled back. "Hearing you say that. Diablo, I never thought a fairy's mouth could be so filthy."

"My thoughts are filthier."

He nibbled along her collarbone. "Tell me."

"Are…are you sure? You're not one for…dirty words."

She felt his smile against her clavicle. "I rather enjoy hearing dirty-mouthed fairies. Go on, baby doll. Tell me."

"Okay."

His teeth grazed her nipple, making her breath catch.

"I was thinking of your cock stretching my pussy like I've never been stretched before."

He growled, and she felt the echo of it tickle against her throat.

"Filling my pussy in a way my dildo never could, in the way I've fantasized about."

He slid a finger inside her.

She arched her back. "Even better than that, and that is"—she moaned as his finger massaged her g-zone—"so good."

"Mm." His lips brushed against her navel.

"I want your cock so deep inside me, Thatch, deeper than anything has ever been, touching parts of me that have never known touch. I want to know it, Thatch. My pussy wants to know it."

Another growl, and he was slipping his finger out of her pussy. He pushed back so he was kneeling between her spread legs. His fingers worked open the drawstrings of her satchel. There was a little tremble to his hands that excited her.

He stared at the shimmering contents inside the bag. "Are you sure it will work if I touch it? My demonic fingers won't jinx the fairy magick?"

"No. Your demonic fingers can touch my fairy dust all they want."

"Why did that sound dirty?"

She only smiled.

Careful, he collected a pinch of her fairy dust between his three fingers. "So…I just…sprinkle it on your…" He stared at her between her legs.

"Thatch, you said it a moment ago."

His gaze met hers. "Pussy."

She shivered. "I like hearing you say it, and, yes, that's all you have to do."

His eyes shifted back down. He reached out and let the glittering sparkles fall from his fingers. They caught the beams of light as the sun rose above the horizon, making them glint brighter on their descent. When they landed on her pussy like warm, golden snowflakes, their magick spread over her and seeped inside. Every bit of her tingled with shimmers. Their touch was like a shot of eroticism straight to her core. She squirmed her hips.

Goddess, she needed him.

"Are you alright?" he asked.

She bit her bottom lip and nodded.

"Now me?"

She nodded again.

His hands lowered to his pants, but she sat up and brushed his hands away so she could undo the button and pull down the zipper. Then she parted the sides to set his cock free. She couldn't stop from licking her lips. What was it about his cock that made her want to taste him? Mouth watering, she leaned forward and licked the top of his cock before swirling her tongue around the head.

"I love your cock," she said.

His fingers combed through her hair.

Eager for more, she dipped her fingers into the satchel resting in his palm. Her dust was soft. Nothing like glitter. It was like touching figments of light, if light had a solid form. Not hot. Not cold. Warm with wonder. She pinched a bit of it and sprinkled it along his length. He sucked in a breath. The fairy dust settled onto his flesh, gleaming brightly and then gradually faded, as if sinking into his body to do its magick.

"Do you think that's enough?"

Thatch's question made her chuckle. To put his mind at ease, she removed a little more from the satchel and let the flecks flutter down to his cock. "Now that's plenty." She took the satchel from him and set it aside. Then she took his shoulders in her hands, guided him down onto her dress, and slung her leg over his hips.

His own wide hands grasped her waist. "Baby, take it slow, and if it hurts—"

"Ssh." And she lowered down. The head of his cock kissed her vulva.

His hands tightened on her. His fingertips dug into her skin.

First, just the wide head nudged into her. There was no resistance. The tip of his cock pushed into her easily. The feel of that stretch skyrocketed her craving for him. She continued to sink onto his cock. He filled her and filled her and filled her some more until she was seated on him.

His chest rose and fell. "Diablo, I never thought I'd be inside you like this. Are you okay?"

"I'm more than okay, Thatch." She rolled her pelvis, taking him yet deeper.

Thatch seethed between his teeth. "You feel so good."

"So do you." She kicked her pace up a notch but faltered, suddenly self-conscious. "Is this…is this right? Am I doing this right?" Sure, he knew she was inexperienced, but she didn't want him to be disappointed.

"Baby doll, you're perfect." He clutched her waist. "So perfect."

She believed him. How could she not when he was looking up at her as if she were the center of the universe. His gaze took all of her in—her breasts swaying with her movements, her stomach as she rocked back and forth, her thighs clenching him, her bare mons pubis, and her face as a moan slipped loose.

He pulled her down so her breasts pressed to his chest and gave her a kiss that left her dazed. His arms locked around her, keeping her against him.

She ground her pelvis, and he lifted his hips to meet her movements. In each other's embrace, they made love in a dew-kissed field as the sun sent stunning slashes of color across the sky and the birds began to sing their praise. Her cries joined their birdsong.

Thatch's cock stroking inside her and her clit rubbing against him created an all-new level of pleasure she'd never experienced before. It was magnificent and all at once too much, but even when she became still in order to grasp him and freefall into the pleasure, he didn't cease his own movements. He drove her over the edge until she shattered on top of him, wailing into his neck. In response, the birds created a chorus to compliment the sound of her ecstasy.

Thatch finished with a roar, pumping her full of his cum, and she wanted nothing more than to take every drop of it. He continued to hold her long after her heart rate had calmed and the birds had settled.

"Aster?"

"Hm?"

He twirled a lock of her hair around his finger. "I call you 'baby doll' every day, but what would you like me to call you when I'm completely, perfectly, and incandescently happy?"

The fact that he was quoting *Pride & Prejudice* in that moment delighted her to no end.

She snuggled into him. "Call me yours."

18

Shake the Enchanted Hierarchy

They'd made love and showered together all before Paisley joined them in the kitchen for breakfast wearing one of Case's shirts cinched at the waist with a belt. She smiled at Thatch. When she looked at Aster, something unspoken passed between best friends, and she winked. That was all she did, though, and Thatch thanked Diablo, because if she'd made a big deal out of the fact that he and Aster had been able to have sex, he would've melted into a purple puddle with just a pair of horns left to indicate a demon had once stood there.

"Coffee smells great. You have no idea the things you miss when..." She headed for the coffeemaker. "...you're kidnapped." The last words were spoken under her breath, but Thatch had caught them, and so had Aster, who'd lowered her face toward her own cup of coffee with generous amounts of sugar and cream.

"I can only imagine how awful it had been," Aster muttered.

Paisley filled her cup with coffee. "The worst part was missing everyone." Her spoon made tinkling sounds against the cup as she stirred in sugar, but the action didn't cover up her next words. "Especially Case."

Paisley and Case had a relationship that Thatch didn't quite understand, but he didn't need to, because it was clear that despite their differences and enjoyment of picking fights, what they had mattered. Nothing had been clearer to Thatch when he attempted to subdue Case during his rampage.

Aster's smile revealed that she'd heard Paisley's words, too. She peered up at Thatch with that sweet little smile.

He shook his head at her, telling her not to think about it. Paisley and Case didn't need either of them meddling in their affairs or thinking things that could pressure either of them.

Aster mouthed, "I'm just happy."

He tweaked her chin. "I know."

Paisley joined them at the table and sipped her coffee. "Now that's heaven."

They were drinking their coffees when Case barged in, looking more terrified than all the other recent occasions for terror. He jolted to a halt. "Oh, goddamn it."

Thatch arched a brow. "Since when do you curse using God's name and not Diablo's?"

"Since now!" Case looked at Paisley a moment. "Excuse me." And he whipped around, escaping as if a hellhound was on his heels.

"What in the world do you think that was about?" Aster asked.

"I think that was about me." Paisley set down her cup. "I'll check on him." She left the kitchen and her coffee behind.

Aster sighed. "Do you think they're going to fight again?"

"Those two? I'd say the odds are good."

Her shoulders lowered.

He rubbed her arm. "They'll be okay, baby doll."

They didn't hear raised voices, but Paisley did return seeking Aster's help. Curious, he followed the two of them to Case's private gym. Case sat on the bench press with busted knuckles. Blood spotted the punching bag.

"Dust his hands," Paisley said to Aster.

Aster took a couple steps.

Case ground out his reply. "My hands are fine."

Aster's fingers stilled as she pulled open her satchel of fairy dust.

"They're not fine."

Aster hopped forward, ready to do her fairy thing.

"I don't need to be healed."

She froze.

"You do, too."

Poor little Aster posed on tiptoe, unsure of whose order to follow.

"My hands have been worse."

Aster peered between them and then glanced over her shoulder at Thatch for help. Unfortunately, going against either of them wouldn't be a good choice. If it were him, he'd chuck some fairy dust at the grumpy bastard and be done with it. Paisley's anger was unpredictable. Case, however, could be brought down with a sweet dimple-framed smile.

"Case, I swear to the Goddess that if you don't let Aster sprinkle some damn fairy dust on your hands, your hands are never going to touch me again."

Thatch knew right then that Paisley had delivered the knockout blow.

Case's eyes blazed gold. Although he was glaring at Paisley, his voice was soft and aimed at Aster. "Cutie pie, can you bless me with a bit of that fairy dust of yours?"

"I'd be happy to." She sprang into action and dusted Case's split knuckles. The bruises,

swelling, and blood vanished.

"Happy?" he spat at Paisley.

"Very. Aster, can you give us some privacy?"

They apparently had no clue Thatch was even in the room.

"Sure." Aster skipped toward him, clearly delighted that the two were going to have it out and no doubt kiss and make up. She snagged his hand

and led him back to the kitchen. “Today has been a wonderful day so far.”

Thatch laughed. “If this is how happy you’ll be, I’ll give you an orgasm every morning and find you someone to heal after our coffee.”

“Sounds amazing.” She bit into a strawberry. “I wonder if they’re going to discuss the Enchanted Hierarchy Ball.” Now her eyes were sparkling. “I brought it up to Paisley yesterday. I told her that I thought Case would want to go with her.”

“Case hates the ball. Usually he just drinks himself stupid, but I have a feeling he’d enjoy the ball much more with Paisley on his arm.”

Her wings fluttered. “I can’t wait to see them at the ball together.”

And she got her wish.

In the blink of an eye, the night of the Enchanted Hierarchy Ball was upon them. Thatch and Case were waiting for the girls at the foot of the stairs. Thatch wore black and white threads. Standing there, he kept shifting back and forth on his feet, fiddling with the cufflinks, and adjusting the black bow tie. He’d never been more uncomfortable in his life, but he’d dress up in an actual monkey suit if it meant spending time with Aster. And dancing with her.

“Will you relax,” Case said. “Aster is going to be beautiful, and she’ll blush down to her toes when she sees you in this getup. Everything is going to be fine.”

Thatch nodded. “At the ball, I usually stand along the wall and watch you drink all the whiskey in the place. I’ve never gone with someone… with someone like…”

"Like her?" Case indicated at the top of the staircase.

Thatch lifted his gaze and was stunned stock-still in the middle of fooling with his tie again. Aster came down a step at a time. She wore a black dress with a tight corset and a full skirt. Orange and black monarch butterflies the size of his hands covered the dress from hips to hem. Smaller butterflies, much closer to the actual size of butterflies, speckled her braided hair. When she paused in front of him and smiled, his attention went to her lips, painted a glossy nude that he desired to kiss until her lips were *really* naked.

Case nudged him.

He cleared his throat. "You look beautiful."

"Do I look too much like a fairy?" She swiped one hand along her skirt and lifted the other to her hair. "Are the butterflies too much?"

"Look as much of a fairy as you want, baby doll. I want everyone there to know I'm with the most beautiful fairy in existence."

And she did blush. Although he couldn't see her toes, Thatch figured Case was right that they were as pink as her cheeks.

He cupped her face. "I am proud to be a demon and to have you on my arm."

She gazed up at him with a sheen of unshed tears over her eyes. "I am proud to be a fairy and to be on your arm."

Heels on the staircase had them turning to see Paisley descending in a gold dress. She paused and tilted her head at Case. "Is this that staircase moment in romance movies where the guy looks up at the girl in awe of her beauty?"

From behind, Thatch studied Case. Oh, yeah, the demon was in awe. He looked about ready to drop to his knees in praise.

Thatch shifted back to Aster. He, himself, was about ready to drop to his knees in praise of the fairy before him.

Aster reached up to right his bowtie. "You look devastatingly handsome."

"I feel like an idiot."

She shook her head. "But you always wear button-up shirts and slacks."

"But I don't wear a bowtie or cufflinks or—" He rolled his shoulders, feeling restricted in the jacket.

"You look amazing, but if it'll help…after the ball, I'll strip you myself."

He blinked. "Can we skip the ball and go right to you stripping me naked?"

And even though it had been her idea, the pink of her cheeks darkened.

Before either of them could say more, Case's words carried to them. "Ready to give the entire Enchanted Hierarchy something to talk about?"

Thatch turned to see Paisley's grin. "Born ready."

Except, no one else at the ball was born ready. They were raised to be prejudiced. They were brought up to believe that it was wrong for two different creatures to love each other. They were molded into the discriminating bastards who eyed them with hate and disgust. He caught their whispers as they walked past them. Cruel whispers about their size difference that reminded Thatch of his own fears. Fears that her fairy dust had vanquished with their sweet magick. Thank Diablo Aster hadn't heard any of the things they were saying now, because if she had, would their first time in the field at sunrise had happened? Or all the spectacular times after that? Or stayed in a relationship with him? Or be there with him right now, holding onto his arm and lowering her head.

He bent his neck to whisper, "Don't listen to them, baby doll."

"Keep whispering to me and I won't be able to hear them."

"Done."

Except right then, Paisley and Case did something that shut everyone up, including Thatch. They engaged in a lip lock in front of all the prying eyes. And that kiss was a clear middle finger up in the air at all those disapproving jerks.

Aster let out a little giggle.

Thatch smirked. "Do I need to cover your eyes from their borderline erotic display of public affection?"

She nudged him. "It's not that. Oh—"

Paisley and Case's kiss became some sort of mating dance with their lips and tongues, and all for everyone to gawk at.

"Alright." Thatch steered Aster away. "That's enough of that."

On the edge of the dance floor, Aster pulled him to a stop. He glanced down at her to see her watching the dancers spinning and twirling and swaying to the waltz emitting from violins played by elves. Demons danced with demons. Fairies with fairies. Vampires with vampires. Elves with elves. Shifters with shifters. And so on.

"Wow." Her voice was a whisper of awe. "I don't fit in here. At all."

Hands on her shoulders, he guided her around to face him. "You don't need to fit in with them. Because you fit right here." He twined his fingers with hers and stepped closer so their bodies touched. "You fit with me."

Her eyes misted. "Don't make me cry with all this makeup on, Thatch."

"I'm sorry, baby, but I don't ever want you to doubt where you belong. None of these people matter. Their opinions, their rules, their cliques, not even their hatred is worth a thing. You're ten times better than all of them put together."

"They're royalty and leaders and the highest of the Enchanted Hierarchy."

"They have nothing on you, baby."

She shook her head.

He bent down to silence her objections with a kiss.

For the second time since they arrived, everyone fell into a stunned hush, but this time it was because of *their* kiss. The tension in Aster's body softened until she was leaning into him, using him for support, and he had no problem holding her up while he kissed her. She lowered from tiptoe, pulling their lips apart. A sigh left her as she laid her cheek on his chest.

He stroked a hand over her back. A glance over her head showed him the women closest to them—vampire, demon, shifter, it didn't matter—were swooning at their display. One had a hand to her chest. Another was fanning herself. All had eyes full of jealousy at what he and Aster had. Suddenly, it didn't matter that he was a demon, and she was a fairy. What mattered was their clear love for each other. They all felt it. He felt it. He just didn't have the nerve to ask Aster if *she* felt it. Sure, she kissed him like she did. Held him like she did. And she claimed she was his, but he had no right to assume she was in love. As in love as he was. He could only hope and wonder if she'd ever say those three words to him, because until she did, he was afraid to voice them first. No, he hadn't been shy about hinting at his feelings, but he couldn't get those three words out unless he knew for sure that she loved him, too.

He inhaled, drawing in her sweet scent. Even if she never said it, he would continue to kiss her like that. He would continue to hold her like this. He would forever love her in all the ways. Even if he had to keep those three words inside.

"Hey, love birds." Wren stepped up to them. He wore a dark metallic suit that made him look more like an ice demon than ever, especially when paired with his white-blue skin and long silver hair. "That was quite a show the two of you put on a moment ago. Case and Paisley would've been a tough act to follow, but I daresay the two of you kissing shocked them more. They expect that sort of thing from the two of them, but another demon and fairy duo? Now that's earth shattering."

Aster stared at the floor. "I don't want to shatter the earth."

Wren gave her a smile. "Perhaps not, but an

interspecies relationship does at least shake the Enchanted Hierarchy."

Thatch glared at Wren. If he had the goal of making Aster second guess their relationship, the look on Aster's face showed it was working.

"And I'm glad for it."

Aster looked up. "You are?"

"Of course I am. Factions are one thing, until it becomes segregating species, and that I can't stand. Case and Paisley, and you and Thatch aren't the only ones who wish for a relationship with someone society says we shouldn't be with." His gaze rose above Aster's head.

Thatch followed his eyeline toward Queen Enya's ward, Seraphina, of the fier faction. She wasn't a dragon shifter, though. In fact, Thatch wasn't sure what she was, but that didn't matter. Not with the way Wren was staring at her. And Thatch could see why. She was stunning with hair like an upside down candleflame—blue to white to yellow and then orange and red. Her skin was sun-kissed golden, and she wore a silvery-blue dress the same color as her roots and Wren's skin. Wren appeared completely taken by her, but the longing in his eyes didn't look new. It spoke of years of quiet pining.

Aster shivered.

Thatch's instincts had him pulling her closer so she could absorb his body heat.

Although small, and although Wren had been watching Seraphina with silent intensity, Wren had noticed. His shoulders lowered a fraction, and he dipped his chin. "I'm sorry," he muttered. "That's me."

And he took a step back.

"Oh, no, it's okay," Aster said while reaching out as if to pull him back to where he'd stood a moment ago. "I'm fine. Honest."

Wren smiled. "You're too kind. I'm good here."

"I want to thank you for everything you've done," she said.

His dark silver brows furrowed. "I haven't done anything."

"But you have. You stayed with the fairy in the woods. Through the whole night. You stayed. That was extremely kind."

"I did what anyone would've done."

She shook her head. "No one would've expected a demon or *anyone* to do that. Only another fairy or elf would understand the importance of that."

Wren shifted as if uncomfortable by her praise. "I did what I would've wanted someone to do for a loved one. She was alone. She shouldn't have been left alone. I couldn't leave her there. Couldn't be heartless like that."

Aster smiled. "You're far from heartless."

He bowed his head again, truly humble. "I'll leave you two lovebirds." His dark blue eyes shifted to Thatch. "A slow song came on. Dance with your pretty fairy."

Aster beamed.

"Do you want to dance, baby doll?"

"I'd love to."

Thatch led her onto the dance floor while Wren went to stand alongside the wall, keeping an eye in the direction of where Seraphina stood behind Queen Enya.

And although she stood in the background, trying to be invisible, she was anything but. She was too beautiful to be able to hide, especially with that hair. It'd be like Aster trying to shrink herself from sight. Wings and all. Impossible.

As he drew Aster to him, he hoped Wren would get this. One day, and one day soon. For now, Thatch was happy that he finally found it himself. And he wouldn't let anything stop him from getting his happy ending with this enchanting creature in his arms, staring up at him with adoring eyes.

Paisley's laughter reached him, and he looked over at Paisley and Case. Maybe the two of them wouldn't get the happy ending that Thatch wanted with Aster. Hell, Thatch had no clue what kind of happy ending they wanted, except the sort that resulted in mind-blowing orgasms. If that was what they wanted, then they should have it. No, they weren't a conventional couple, but they worked, and to Thatch, the fact they worked counted for something. Something big.

Paisley's laughter cut short, and she stilled.

Thatch's brows lowered.

She'd seemed to be enjoying herself a moment ago, but that joy was draining away from her face. Her body jerked, and she seemed to slump in Case's arms. A spot of red in the middle of Paisley's back caught Thatch's attention as it grew across the gold fabric of her dress.

"Cover!"

Case's order had Thatch's wings springing out of his body and curling around Aster to shield her. He didn't even have to think. The instinct to protect was automatic. At the same time, he swept Aster into his arms and hunkered low to the ground to cradle her as close to him as he could.

The force of the bullets ramming against his wings slid him back a few inches on the tile. Grinding his teeth, growling in his throat, he held on and put all of his weight down to keep the bullets from shoving him even more.

Aster clutched his suit jacket. "What's happening?"

"Shh. It's okay. I've got you."

Not a single bullet would get through to harm her. His wings could handle a lot without receiving so much as a scratch, but if his wings *did* happen to fail, he'd spin around and put his own back in the line of fire. The bullets would pepper his back. Eventually, the gunshots would prove fatal, but he'd die if it meant she'd live. He'd be her armor even in death.

"Thatch. Is Paisley…?" Her voice gave out.

"I don't know."

The bullets striking his wings and falling to the tile created a deafening din. Inside the cocoon of his wings, darkness surrounded him. A dozen things he wanted to say to Aster were on the tip of his tongue. First and last were the three words he couldn't get out—I love you.

But they had time. He'd make sure they'd have time later. Yes—he held her tighter—he'd tell her later. No matter what. Even if she didn't say it first. He had to gather his courage and voice his truth, like his grandfather had done before him.

"Case! The coast is clear."

Wren's shout had Thatch opening his wings slowly to see that he hadn't been the only one to cover a fairy. Every demon there had done the same. Not a single fairy had been harmed.

"Thatch!"

He rotated to see that Case and Paisley may not have time later. Blood had created a puddle beneath Paisley, and more fell from two streams at her back.

"Get her to safety."

Thatch lifted Aster and ran with her toward the exit.

"Wait. No. I can heal her now. Please. She's dying."

"At Case's," was all he said before launching into the air.

He made it to Case's in under a minute flat.

Aster yanked on the ties to her satchel to rip it off her waist. "She was shot." Her voice shook. "Paisley was shot. Who would do that? Who…?"

Thatch grabbed her shoulders. "Breathe, baby, breathe."

"I can't breathe, Thatch. I'm scared. She could die. She could be dead right now. If she dies—"

"She won't. She's strong. She's a fighter."

The front door banged open.

Case rushed inside carrying Paisley. "Aster!"

"Here, here." She tugged open the satchel as Case dropped to his knees.

Thatch stepped up to them. Seeing Paisley colorless from blood loss, her lips blue, was wrong. She was a queen. She was supposed to be vibrant. Not limp. Not pale as death crept upon her. Not bleeding out in his best friend's arms.

Aster doused Paisley's wounds with generous pinches of fairy dust.

The gunshot wounds sealed, and the blood on Paisley's skin vanished.

Thatch and Aster followed Case into the parlor where he laid Paisley on the couch. Paisley didn't so much as stir. Her head lolled to the side on the armrest.

"She lost a lot of blood," Aster said while gently adjusting Paisley's head.

Case removed his jacket and worked up his sleeve. "You know what to do."

Thatch stood back as Aster slipped an IV into Paisley's vein and attached the other end to Case's arm. Aster's question returned to him. Who would do this? They had thought they'd eliminated the threat after killing the vampires in the cave.

But they'd been wrong.

19

Most Ardently

Soon after she'd set Case up to give Paisley blood, Jude and Lena arrived.

"Is she okay?" Jude looked toward the parlor where Case knelt on the floor beside the couch that Paisley's dress spilled off of.

"I healed her," Aster said. "Case is giving her blood. She's okay."

Jude's hooves scraped against the tile when he took a tiny step forward. "How can Case do that? Give her blood?"

"He's a universal donor." Aster glanced at Case as he adjusted the tube that connected him to Paisley. "His blood is the only blood she needs."

Jude's body shivered. "I've failed her. Her father named me her godfather so I could protect her if he wasn't around. And here she almost died on my watch."

Aster laid a hand on his side. "You didn't fail. None of this is your fault. No one could've known this would happen. No one. Not you. Not Case. Not Paisley."

"I've known her since she was born, and I almost saw her die. It shouldn't be like that. We shouldn't ever have to see someone die who we saw born."

Aster rubbed the shoulder of his horse body. "She's okay."

He shifted toward her. "Are *you* okay? We were outside. I saw the aftermath of the attack. According to people who were inside at the time, they targeted every fairy there, but more so Paisley and you."

"I'm okay."

"Good. I don't know what I'd do if both of you were hurt." He tugged playfully on one of her braided hair loops. "I've known you since you were a tiny thing with wings that could barely lift you."

Paisley's family had always been her family, from the time she'd met Paisley at the thatch in the woods. Recalling that day brought a smile to Aster's face. She'd lost her own family from iron poisoning when she was little and had been taken in by Mum. But Paisley's parents had always treated her like a daughter; Paisley had said they were sisters from minute one, and Jude had doted on her as much as Paisley.

A knock at the door stopped her from saying anything that probably would've made Jude uncomfortable.

"May I get that?" Lena asked.

"Please."

Lena opened the door, and Wren stood there. "Zara has called an emergency meeting tomorrow because of the attack," he said. "All faction leaders are to be there." He peered toward the parlor. "Paisley, too, if she survives."

Aster swallowed. "She will."

The bullets had gone straight through.

The iron hadn't been in her body long.

The wounds were healed.

And Case was replenishing the blood she'd lost.

So, Aster had to believe that everything was fine and Paisley would survive this. She had to. For the vampyre faction. For the faye faction. For Aster.

For Case.

Paisley *had* to live.

Wren bowed his head. "Of course she will. I have to go. Silas has requested to speak to one of Case's council members." He met Thatch's eye, who stood back, keeping an eye on Case and Aster. "I figured you'd want to stay here."

"You figured right."

"I'll return after I speak to Silas." Wren opened the door to find Phoenix there. "Phoenix." He bowed.

"Oh, Wren!" She snatched him up into a hug.

"Careful, love. I'm too cold for you."

She stepped back and rolled her eyes. "I'm a dragon shifter, Wren. Remember? My blood runs hotter than most."

Still, he edged around her. "I do remember that. I have to speak to Silas."

Aster started toward Wren, but Phoenix had shut the door. Just like when he'd found the fairy in the woods and stayed there through the night, he did things without even thinking about his safety because he was duty-bound. After people had unleashed hundreds of bullets at a public event, she wanted to tell him to be careful. He looked out for them, but no one was looking out for Wren. So, she wanted to do that, except he was already gone.

Phoenix hurried over to Aster. "Tell me she's alive."

"She is. Case is with her."

Phoenix sighed. "Thank all the goddesses."

"Would your mother be thankful?" Jude asked Phoenix. "Or would she be disappointed?"

Lena touched his arm. "Jude."

Phoenix, though, didn't bat a lash. "I don't blame you for asking me that. My mother is many things, but she's not the type to hire assassins or commit cold-blooded murder. She was terrified when the shooting started. She pushed me and Sera to the floor, thinking we were going to get shot. So, yes, my mother is many things, says many things, and does *many* questionable things, but this wasn't her."

Lena stroked Jude's arm. "I believe her."

"So do I," Aster said.

Phoenix shrugged a shoulder. "He doesn't have to believe me if he wants to."

Jude sighed. "You've always been a good girl. I believe you."

Phoenix grinned. "Well, I'm not *always* a good girl." And she gave him a wink.

Another knock on the front door sounded.

"I've got it." Phoenix opened the door to Wren. "That was quick."

"No time to waste." He stepped inside but stayed a couple of feet from everyone. "Silas said the faye faction is on lockdown."

Aster's eyes widened. "Goddess, I haven't even thought of the faye faction." Which, in her mind, only proved she'd be a terrible leader.

"They're alright. Case already had a plan in place in the event of danger. Demons deployed to the faye faction the instant a threat was detected. I checked myself. The faye faction is surrounded. And Silas has sent vampires out to search the area. I need to talk to Case about sending demons out to join them." He looked toward the parlor. "Should I interrupt?"

Thatch inclined his head. "He'd want an update."

"Right." Wren went over, hands clasped behind his back, and kept distance between him and Case as he spoke softly. A moment later, he stepped out of the parlor to speak to Thatch. "I'm going to send demons to join the search party. I'll return once they're gone."

Now was Aster's chance.

She hurried over to him when he opened the front door. "Wren."

He paused.

"Be careful. Okay?"

"I'm just going to issue our best demons an order."

"Still. Be careful."

He smiled. "I'll be back in a moment."

And he did return, with a message that twenty demons were now joining forces with dozens of vampires on the hunt for who had tried to assassinate the vampyre-faye queen.

"The odds of them finding the fuckers who did this are slim."

They all turned toward the voice.

Case was fixing his sleeve in the entrance to the parlor. "They were probably long gone by the time Thatch left with Aster."

On the couch, Paisley was still unconscious.

"You have to have faith," Aster told him.

"Your faith is going to have to work for the both of us." He peered over his shoulder at Paisley. "I don't want to go far, but you all can go into the conference room. Let me know if you hear anything or come up with anything."

One by one, they filed into the conference room.

Aster stared after Case as he paced the length of the parlor. He and Paisley would probably die before calling each other boyfriend and girlfriend, but there was no denying that they had something special. Questionable at times, but special.

Thatch rubbed her arms. "Come on, baby doll. Let's give him privacy."

"Right." Case probably wouldn't want anyone watching him pace and worry and occasionally mumble curses under his breath. "You're right."

In the conference room, discussions about what they should do and who could be behind this attack got underway. Aster wasn't paying attention to any of it. Her thoughts were with Paisley and Case in that parlor. Paisley should've woken up by now. Even with the blood loss, she'd expected Paisley to come to, even briefly. But not even after Case had given her his own blood had she so much as stirred.

Aster wrung her hands. That faith she was supposed to have was dwindling rapidly.

This was one of the times she wished she were stronger, braver, bigger. Strong like Case. Brave like Paisley. Big like Thatch. She was nothing but a fairy who had to be shielded and carried and left behind.

The conference room door opened.

The discussion around her fell silent.

Aster gasped when Paisley walked in.

Aster popped to her feet and launched herself at Paisley. Probably with a little too much enthusiasm considering Paisley had just been unconscious and still might be feeling the lingering effects of blood loss, but her happiness at seeing Paisley on her feet couldn't be contained. Paisley knocked backward into Case when Aster slammed into her for a hug.

"Damn, cutie pie," Case said. "You may be tiny but you can tackle like no other."

Paisley laughed softly as she returned the hug.

Aster inched back to get a good look at Paisley. Her coloring was back with pink cheeks and rose-colored lips. "That was scary."

"I know." Paisley squeezed her hands. "Are you okay? Were you hit?"

"No. The second Case shouted for cover, Thatch surrounded me with his wings." And she'd felt so safe in his embrace.

Paisley's gaze lifted above Aster's head, and Aster read her lips. "Thank you."

One of Thatch's hands curled around Aster's shoulders, and he pulled her gently to him. She tipped her head back to see Thatch give Paisley a nod that said so much more than that subtle movement.

Jude stepped up to them.

Aster backed away to give godfather and goddaughter space.

Jude snatched Paisley up into a hug that brought Paisley onto tiptoe. "Don't scare us like that."

"I'm sorry." Paisley rubbed his arm. "That wasn't my intention." She peered around at all of them gathered in the conference room. "Where's Silas?"

Case hooked an arm around Paisley's waist. "He's leading a group of vampires, joined with a team of demons. They're searching for the culprits who did this."

The shock on Paisley's face was clear as day. "Vampires and demons are working together?"

"For you, they are, but I don't think they're going to be successful."

That was the cloud hanging over all their heads. Somehow, they'd all been tricked into believing they'd eliminated the threat, only for Paisley to almost lose her life. Now, they knew the truth. The culprits who had tried to kill Paisley, murdered two fairies, and threatened Aster's life were still out there. But none of them knew who they were. The chances of finding them were growing smaller with the more time that went by.

"Which is why we're here." Jude crossed his arms. "Zara called an emergency meeting tomorrow. This shit has gone on too long. We have to end it."

Wren spoke from his place at the table. "Here in this room, there's four faction leaders. Five, really, because of you. Plus, two more demons, the fier faction's heir, and a fairy ready to fight."

Aster smiled, thrilled to have been included and deemed a fighter by a demon who was one of Case's top men.

"What can we do?" he asked.

"Use me as bait."

The bit of pride Aster had felt diminished at Paisley's words.

Case's voice cut through the blistering silence. "Excuse me?"

Aster took a teensy step back into Thatch to get out of the way in case the two of them started to fight.

"Hear me out." Even though Paisley looked at them, Aster understood each word was weighed carefully and for Case, who was stalking around her, eying her with eyes glowing gold. "They want me, and they want me to give up my thrones. We can use this as a tipping point, as the thing that breaks me." Case stopped in front of Paisley, and Thatch drew Aster back another step. "We stage a falling out," Paisley said to Case. "At the meeting tomorrow. In front of everyone, we have a blow up. We make it good. If we succeed in convincing the faction leaders that we're over, then all the factions will know about it within an hour. I'll go home, and you'll pull back your demons. Whoever is behind this will take the bait knowing you won't be around to protect me."

Except they all knew that there was no way Case wouldn't be around to protect her. Not after he had failed to protect her when she'd needed it the most. And he vowed it right then and there. Paisley would put on an act, and Case would be right there, ready to take on the bastards who'd hurt his queen, and so would Aster.

Aster couldn't stop her feet from pacing the length of Case's parlor. It was all she could do while wondering what was unfolding at the emergency Enchanted Hierarchy Council Meeting. Paisley and Case were supposed to be putting on a good show of ending things in front of all the faction leaders. Only Jude and Lena would know the truth, that the two of them were more together now than ever before.

"Aster, come here."

She turned to Thatch.

He sat on the couch, holding his hand out to her. "Stop pacing, baby doll. Come here."

She went to him and laid her hand in his.

He coaxed her onto his lap. "Why are you so wound up, love?"

"I'm worried. I wish we were there. We should've gone. And why aren't you wound up and pacing? Pace with me, damn it."

Thatch chuckled. “With the way you were pacing, you were going to carve out a path in the floor. This is Paisley’s plan. We have to trust them. And wait.”

She pouted, hoping to hit him with something he usually caved to.

“Keep pouting like that, and I’ll do something to your mouth that will have you far from pouting.”

She gaped, not prepared to hear anything like that coming from Thatch’s mouth. But holy Goddess, he knew how to say vaguely naughty things in a growly voice that gave her tingles everywhere.

He grinned. “Did I shock you?”

“Y-yes.”

“Good. Don’t forget it.”

She likely never would.

The front door opened.

Aster sprang to her feet.

Case came in. From where she stood, she could tell his body was tense. “The plan is a go. Everyone at the meeting was convinced of our falling out.” He pulled his phone from his pocket. “I have to call Paisley. The end of our public fight was…I have to make sure she’s okay. Our men around her property are pulling back. Thatch, you need to get into position now. I don’t know if her kidnappers will act so quickly but—”

Thatch stood. “We’re not going to take that chance.”

Case nodded. “Wren is going to stay here with you, cutie pie.”

She frowned as Wren entered. So now she needed a babysitter?

"I know that look. That's the look of a woman about to be stubborn. And that's my cue to call the Queen of Stubbornness. Excuse me." Case left while tapping on the screen of his phone.

Poor Wren looked like he wanted a reason to leave and shuffled his way back toward the door.

Thatch took her shoulders in his hands. "Promise me you're going to stay here."

She bit her tongue.

"Promise me, baby. You need to stay here with Wren. Where it's safe." He lifted a hand to her cheek. "I can only leave if I know you're going to be safe. I'll only be able to do what I need to do, and look out for Paisley, if I don't have to worry about you being in danger, too. Please stay here."

She sighed and laid her hand over his. "Okay, but you have to promise me something."

"What?"

"I need you to be careful."

"Baby doll, we don't know what kind of people we'll be up against."

She curled her fingers in his shirt. "Which is why I need you to be careful."

"I will." He kissed her forehead. "I have to go."

She nodded.

When he started to turn, she grabbed him and tugged him down to kiss him on the mouth. Then she shoved him. "Okay. Go. Quickly."

Jaw clenched, shoulders squared, he marched out the door.

Then the slap of his wings beating against the air sounded.

Moments later, Case headed for the door. He'd ditched his tie and jacket. "I'll call with an update," he told Wren.

Wren inclined his head. "I'll wait for word."

Case didn't even spare her a glance on his way out.

She stood in front of the parlor's windows to see him fly toward Paisley's. He was out of sight in seconds, and with him, he took her last bit of calm.

Wren stepped closer. "They'll all be okay."

"You don't know that. They set Paisley on fire, kidnapped and tortured her, and then shot her full of iron bullets. And let's not forget they murdered two fairies." She crossed her arms to hug herself. "Sawed their wings right off their backs."

"I know." His shoulders lowered. "I'm sorry for all of it. We all wish we could've done more then. This is Paisley, Case, and Thatch doing more *now*."

Wren's words rang true.

She wished she could've done more then.

She wanted to do more now.

Why did the three of them have to do everything themselves?

Why couldn't she help?

She didn't want to be a burden. Or coddled. Or bubble-wrapped like she could shatter at the slightest touch. She wanted to be brave and selfless and badass. Especially now that the people she loved the most were putting themselves in jeopardy. If they were going to be in the line of danger, then that's where Aster wanted to be. Right there in that line with them. Standing shoulder to shoulder. Fighting side by side.

Turning away from the window, she forced her wings to keep from revealing her emotions. "I'm going to try to relax in my room."

Wren bowed his head. "Let me know if you need anything."

She hated deceiving him. Wren was sweet. If he knew what she was planning, he'd do the right thing and stop her, so she had no choice but to lie. "Thank you."

On her way up the stairs, she moved slowly, cautiously, controlling her wings so they wouldn't betray her. She even opened her door as if she were sneaking into her own bedroom. Good thing Wren wasn't following her because he'd know she was up to something by her demeanor. She eased her door closed and tiptoed over to her dresser. Biting her bottom lip, she slid open her panty drawer, where she thought it would make sense to stash her pouch of spikes and blow dart.

With the pouch fastened at her waist, she continued to her balcony. She opened the door, being as quiet as possible. No demons circled the property as they once had. To make it seem like they didn't feel threatened, Case ordered them to stand down. So, Aster was in the clear when she flew off the balcony and pushed her wings to carry her as quickly as possible to Paisley's. She scanned the area around Paisley's property. If Case and Thatch were hidden, she couldn't spot them, which was the point. They couldn't let Paisley's kidnappers know they were there.

She landed on a patch of clover near the edge of the woods. Behind the thick trunk of an oak tree, she peeked out, searching for any sign of movement. Nothing along the woods. Nothing in the gardens. Nothing near the wisteria tree.

She snuck out from behind the oak and made her way cautiously across the yard. The entire way, she was on alert. Eyes peeled. Ears straining. Wings stiff. When she got closer to Paisley's, thumps and thuds reached her ears.

She flinched to a halt.

The front windows were smashed.

Staying as low as she could, she crept to the demolished window.

"Rumor is my father's Diablo himself. I'll make sure you're tortured in the most excruciating ways for all eternity."

Case's threat had her squeezing past holly bushes in front of the windows.

"Is that a promise?"

Her eyes widened. That was unmistakably Silas, Paisley's uncle. She poked her head up to see Case stalking toward Silas with rage radiating off him.

"That's a fucking vow," he spat.

Case stood several paces away from where Silas had a knife to Paisley's throat. Behind him, Thatch was stiff-backed and vibrating with tension.

Silas forced Paisley farther from them, step by step. Lacerations covered her arms and legs, leaking blood across her skin. More blood seeped out from beneath the blade pressed to her neck, a hair's width from her carotid artery.

All this time, the person who wanted Paisley dead was her own uncle?

No, Silas wasn't blood to Paisley, but he had been her father's best friend. They'd become vampires together by the then vampire king. Silas had treated Paisley favorably. But that apparently had all been a lie. He wouldn't have a knife to Paisley's throat now if he loved Paisley. Her three cousins, all turned vampire by Silas, wouldn't be lying dead on the floor, if he hadn't viewed Paisley as a threat, someone he needed to eliminate to get what he coveted, which apparently was the throne to the vampyre faction.

Aster had secretly disliked Silas since she met him. It was the way he smiled. It reminded her of a snake. A fairy's instinct was usually spot on, but she'd buried her unease out of friendship. Perhaps if she hadn't, Paisley's life wouldn't be at stake right now. Paisley wouldn't have experienced any of the trauma she'd endured over the past couple of months.

If only she'd said something!

Silas whispered something in Paisley's ear that Aster couldn't hear.

Case surged forward.

Silas yanked Paisley backward. "I told you to watch it, lover demon." He forced Paisley down. "On your knees."

As if she were giving up, Paisley lowered onto a puddle of blood that had collected at her feet.

"Bring out your wings."

Paisley didn't move. "No."

"Bring out your fucking wings!"

Paisley's wings erupted from her body. They were beautiful. Like black lace. And Silas had a knife to them.

Thatch grabbed Case, keeping him back.

But no one was there to hold Aster back.

She snatched spikes from her pouch.

"Do you have any last words for each other?" Silas asked.

Paisley's words to Case came to Aster through the window as she pushed spikes into her dart with shaking fingers. "Remember that vampire-demon war I threatened you with when we first met?"

Aster lifted the loaded dart.

"You better win it."

She brought the dart to her mouth and aimed.

Paisley closed her eyes.

Aster blew through the tube, adjusted, and blew again, sending two spikes through the air.

A millisecond later, Silas and Paisley flew backward.

Aster climbed through the window and rushed right past Case and Thatch to where Paisley lay on the floor. When Paisley opened her eyes, all Aster said in way of an explanation was, "I never liked your uncle." That would have to do for now because Paisley was still losing blood. She extracted a handful of fairy dust from her satchel and doused Paisley with it.

Her wounds healed, and Paisley sat up. When she looked at her uncle, Aster spared him a glance. The spikes were embedded in his eyes, exactly where she had intended for them to go.

"Holy Goddess, Aster."

Before she could say more, large, warm hands grasped her shoulders. In the next moment, she was plastered against Thatch's chest.

Fear leaked off him in waves, but stronger than that fear was love. "You were supposed to stay home!"

She could understand that Thatch wasn't mad at her for deceiving them when she'd promised to stay home. It was that *and* his love that caused Thatch's voice to rise.

"I wasn't going to stay home when everyone I care about is here. All three of you should've realized that."

Just like she should've realized that he loved her as much as she loved him, and it was about time that she told him.

"And I love you, too."

But perhaps she shouldn't have told him that *he* loved *her* before he could say it himself.

"What?"

Still, it was obvious, and if he wasn't going to tell her, then she'd help him along. She touched his cheek. "I love you, too, you big dummy."

She wasn't expecting the kiss that Thatch drew her into, not with Paisley and Case watching, but the kiss ignited every part of her being. She couldn't stop from squirming in his arms so she could clench his waist with her thighs. Thatch hefted her higher up his body, causing Thatch's clothes to rub against her crotch. Even through her cotton, the friction had her gasping.

"Okay, whoa," Case said. "I don't want to see that."

One of Thatch's arm left her body, a slap of wings unfurling sounded, and he began to move, jostling her with each step. He hadn't stopped kissing her, though, and she was glad.

"Wait, Case has a dagger in his back!"

He does?

Aster couldn't think beyond that because Thatch's tongue stroked against hers, silencing her fairy instinct to heal Case.

His fingers fiddled between them.

The weight of her pouch containing her fairy dust lifted away.

A plop sounded.

She would've told Thatch that it wasn't kind to take a fairy's dust from them, but it was in good hands, and *Thatch's* hands were groping her ass.

Outside, he only stopped kissing her to launch straight up and fly her home. Once they reached Case's, they resumed kissing. He carried her to his room, with their lips connected the entire time. It was any wonder that he didn't trip. If he had, she would've just straddled him right where they landed. Fortunately, he got them all the way to his bed where he laid her down and settled on top of her.

She enjoyed feeling him on top of her. His weight. His warmth. His everything. She wanted this every night, and not even for sex. She just wanted him close. To be in his arms. To hear his breathing. To feel his body heat. To know that he was there and wouldn't ever leave her.

He kissed her as if he could lose himself in her, and she wished he could. Would. She yearned for him to be inside her in every way possible.

He placed a kiss at the pulse in her neck and stayed there a moment, feeling the beats against his lips. She wondered if he could tell when her pulse quickened, because it had. While his lips praised that spot, her heart had picked up pace. Then he trailed kisses down her neck to her collarbone. One hand reached up to slip the strap from her shoulder, and he kissed the curve.

Before Paisley had called for Aster to meet her bodyguard, she never would've thought that a demon could kiss her body like this—worshipful and affectionate. She never would've thought that a demon *could* love her. In fact, she hadn't thought love was in the cards for her because no one had ever stirred her, but Thatch was *made* to love her. She believed that with every fiber of her fairy being. The moment she'd laid eyes on Thatch, her heart had known he was the one, and she was the one for him.

No, she never would've thought she'd be in love with a demon, but she thanked the Goddess for him and for what they had. And she thanked the Goddess he was with her now, planting a kiss in the middle of her palm. Her fingers curled in, holding that kiss there, never wanting to let it go.

Thatch peeled the satin bodice down her chest and peppered kisses along the skin he uncovered. Each kiss was like a devotion. She felt it deep in her skin. He was just as grateful that she was there with him, accepting his love and giving all of hers in return.

His mouth closed around her breast. She'd never get over how intimate that act was. It made her skin break out in gooseflesh and her heart swell with so many emotions that she couldn't describe. At the same time, her pussy throbbed with longing and anticipation of more.

As he nudged her nipple with his tongue, his hand slipped under her dress and pulled her panties down her thighs. She wiggled, assisting him in stripping away the damp cotton.

Thatch spoke against her breast. “Aster, baby, I’d kiss all the rest of you, but I can’t wait any longer.” He raised his head. “I need you. After we could’ve lost Paisley, after you literally saved the day, after you said…” He inhaled. “After you said what I’ve been dying to hear you say, I need you now.”

Nodding, she framed his face with her hands. “I love you, and I need you now, too.”

It was her third time saying it, and she planned to say it thousands of more times. Except, he hadn’t said the words to her. And he still didn’t as he opened his pants and eased inside her.

She couldn’t stop the gasp from leaving her. Not because there was any pain whatsoever, but because it just felt so good to have him inside her. When he filled her completely, she exhaled, as if she were exhaling all her past lonely nights, all the times she’d been jealous of other couples, all her failed attempts at an orgasm, and the belief that she’d be like Mum, mother and grandmother to all but with no partner or children of her own.

Thatch’s cock almost slid all the way out of her as he reversed, and then glided back in, and she inhaled the deeper he went, taking in far more than his flesh but his promises and hopes and dreams. He didn’t have to voice them for her to know each and every one. They were promises, hopes, and dreams that she shared, and she raised her hips the next time he sank into her, so he could get everything he offered her in that moment right back from her. Their movements were in perfect rhythm, their breaths in sync.

With each stroke, her love swelled larger and larger inside her, mixing with the pleasure that bloomed, all warm and swirling. The whole time, he hadn't taken his eyes off her, and she didn't look away, either. Not even when her breath fluttered in and out of her mouth. Not even when she sighed and moaned and cried. Not even when her vision blurred and darkened.

"That's it, baby doll, come for me."

She let out a whimper as her orgasm neared. What he was doing went from incredible to phenomenal to heavenly. She had no choice but to come exactly like how he'd requested. Her orgasm came like a detonation. A wail left her mouth. Followed by another. And another until he shook above her, let out a deep grunt, and filled her with everything he had, everything he was. She liked that sensation, him giving her himself—his past, present, and future.

He rolled off her but took her with him, keeping her firmly to his side.

Her heart raced from their lovemaking.

They both panted.

She lay in his arms more content than ever in her life. Paisley was safe. The bad guys were truly and officially gone. Case could be happy again. And so could Paisley. The two of them had each other. Nothing more stood in their way. They certainly wouldn't let the Enchanted Hierarchy have a say anymore or ever again.

And neither would Thatch or Aster.

Drowsy from the dose of serotonin released by her orgasm, she traced the veins in his arm and thought about how Thatch didn't have to be her bodyguard anymore. They could also have a relationship free of threats and the nagging 'what if' questions. Thatch could be happy, and so could she.

"Aster?"

She kept her eyes closed. "Hm?"

"I love you." Thatch's arms tightened around her. "Most ardently."

Her heart was racing again. She'd been waiting for the moment when he'd finally express his love for her verbally, but the reality was infinity better than she'd ever imagined; he'd freaking quoted *Pride & Prejudice*.

She raised onto her elbow and skimmed his jawline with a fingertip. "I love you, too."

Now, it made sense for her to say 'too', and that single word was stronger than the three that came before it, because it meant those prior words were shared, reciprocated. But it wasn't better than her next two words that were a declaration, a confession, a passionate statement from her heart to his. "Most ardently."

About the Author...

Love Fey is author Chrys Fey's pen name for all the smutty romance stories her muse insists she needs to write. And who is she to go against her muse?

Each story is a spicy love letter to readers looking for book boyfriends and girlfriends of all kinds.

Fey's characters all have a bit of herself in them, whether that's her Arian fire or chronic pain. And every story includes something she loves—nutcrackers, Halloween, references to *Pride & Prejudice* and *Pretty Woman*, witches, gargoyles, and more.

She's a proud cat mama, a nail polish junkie, and will always write and publish romance no matter who may be against it. In fact, if a story idea may get close-minded individuals mad, that story moves to the top of her list.

Website:
LoveFey.com

www.ingramcontent.com/pod-product-compliance
Lightning Source LLC
LaVergne TN
LVHW090557110826
845146LV00001B/168

9798994628256